BOMB SCARE

"Now!" Carter yelled. He took a deep breath and let the small bomb drop on the floor in front of him.

One of the men made a grab for Nick but his lungs were already full of the gas. Carter sat, easily holding his breath while they fell, one by one.

One man remained. He was a bull of a man, and looked like a Georgian farmhand or a circus strongman. Carter came up out of the chair and sank his fist in the man's stomach. It was like hitting a stone wall.

The human tank came at him.

The Killmaster's hand reached out for something to use as a weapon. His right hand found a chair leg, and the young giant went down gulping his last breath.

NICK CARTER IS IT!

FROM THE NICK CARTER
KILLMASTER SERIES

SINGAPORE SLING

KILL MASTER
NICK CARTER

JOVE BOOKS, NEW YORK

KILLMASTER #258: SINGAPORE SLING

A Jove Book/published by arrangement with
The Condé Nast Publications, Inc.

PRINTING HISTORY
Jove edition/February 1990

ISBN: 0-515-10248-2

*Dedicated to the men and women of the
Secret Services of the
United States of America*

SINGAPORE SLING
KILL MASTER

ONE

The chair was custom-made, reinforced to take its owner's weight. It could swivel to cover 360 degrees of the unique room, and tilt to act as a temporary bed for a man who seldom left that room.

He sat, his huge buttocks filling the oversize chair to overflowing, his meaty hands working at switches and keyboards, his eyes never leaving the countless monitors that watched over his empire twenty-four hours a day.

The watching had become an obsession. His conglomerate of banks, shipping lines, warehousing, and the long list of companies in illicit trade, had become too cumbersome to oversee in person, and he had become too fat to move around.

The table was octagonal, the chair in its center. No break in the table and its array of controls allowed for the exit of the gargantuan man. For the few hours a day he left the room, the chair and the floor around it sank slowly to the floor below, controlled smoothly by hydraulic cylinders.

Arthur Cecil Chen, a name given to him by Occidental foster parents, sat in the huge swivel chair. Fat Chen, as he was known to his enemies, patiently moved beady black eyes, set well back in a huge, polished dome of a skull, as he watched one monitor after the other. Ears, small and almost concealed by the rolls of fat, listened to countless conversations. Cameras were set up in every office of any importance in his vast empire. His key people wore concealed cameras designed by an electronics genius under his control. He could hear every conversation by merely flipping a switch. He could, and did, record and file hundreds of thousands of feet of video tape to use as a lever against his enemies. He could interrupt and countermand the orders of his subordinates in his booming voice, a sound that filled the room and matched, in decibels, the almost seven hundred pounds of his weight.

A half dozen of the countless monitors followed robot sentries as they patrolled the perimeter fence around his five-acre estate off Lady Hill Road just north of the Pakistani embassy. Chen was a fanatic about security but would have no human agents in the house. Human betrayal was his only fear. He was paranoid about other humans coming near him. One man served his every need, a small Malayan who had been with Chen for so long he could usually anticipate the big man's every wish.

Just as he was about to shake the walls with a bellow for food, a huge tray descended from the ceiling, covered with a multitude of dishes. It stopped a couple of inches above the array of keyboards, the aroma from steaming plates filling the room.

Heu Choy, his man, was an accomplished cook, but he

often sent out for native dishes. Feeding the monster who was his master, with all his other duties, was sometimes an overwhelming task. The tray held a cauldron of soup, overflowing platters of smoked Szechuan duck on a bed of fried rice, minced pork with bean curd, lamb in brown sauce with scallions, steamed chicken in lotus leaves, fried eel in garlic sauce, plates of stir-fried vegetables, baskets of fruit.

Fat Chen tied a huge bib around his nonexistent neck to cover the front of the long loose gown he invariably wore. While he moved both hands from the dishes to his mouth, each hand adept at the use of chopsticks, small shovels that kept a steady stream of food going in one direction, the man's dark eyes focused on the monitors that were designed for the guarding of his house. A dozen robots moved in their inexorable patterns, some inside the grounds, others in the double width of fencing surrounding the five acres. The two fences, twelve feet apart, were crisscrossed with laser beams programmed to stop any intruder yet allow passage of the wheeled robots on a very precise computerized program.

Each robot was a marvel—invented by Chen's electronics genius—impersonal, mobile, and deadly. They were about four feet tall, traveled on four wheels over any terrain, and were armed with both laser beams and conventional small arms in domed, rotating heads: four lasers, three 40mm machine guns. No one had attempted to penetrate the fortress. The twin fences were deterrent enough, but the robots, highly visible, made it impossible to approach the house by land or air.

The food was gone in minutes. The tray ascended to the room above while another descended, providing finger bowls and a roll of paper towels.

Finished with his snack, Chen flipped a switch and broke into a conversation in one of his warehouses. "You procrastinate," he charged the three men sitting in a corner office. "The two are obviously foreign agents, probably American. Have you no plans?"

"Kill them, Excellency," one man said.

Chen fumed behind his desk. "You have no imagination. We want no foreign deaths traced back to us. Fools! I have fools working for me!"

"What do you propose, Excellency?" another of the men asked. They were obviously afraid of their employer, of the hold he had over them. He could have them killed in a dozen ways, or a few words in the right ear and they would be jailed for life.

"Set them up. Lead them to Kuala Lumpur. Get them far from our operation and let the local police there deal with them," the booming voice attacked their ears.

"If we have your permission, we could lose a kilo, plant it on them. Do we have your permission?" the third man asked, a haunting fear evident in his voice.

"Must it be a whole kilo?"

"Insurance, Excellency. That much leaves no doubt. Casual users don't carry a whole kilo."

"Good. What is one kilo if we get them off our backs? Just do it and make it fast," Chen said, his voice menacing. "And remember, I am watching you. I won't tolerate failure in this. They have to go and it must be clean. I don't want this coming back to my doorstep."

"Yes, Excellency," they said, in unison.

Fat Chen cut them off with a flick of a chubby finger, then flipped another switch. "Farben. Come to the camera."

A thin face appeared on a screen. The man's teeth were

discolored and stained from cigarettes, and the sparse mustache beneath a long, narrow nose was yellow. His slanted eyes were rheumy, wet at the corners, bloodshot. Behind him, a giant of a man, also Chinese, stood mute, his face dull and expressionless, a human robot, limited but useful in his own way.

"I want you two observing our operation at the Neil Road warehouse. My people there have a disposal job. I don't want any foul-ups. Keep an eye on them."

"Do you have information that will help?" the thin man asked.

"They will be ridding us of a couple of agents who have been nosing around. Make sure they do a clean job for us. Keep out of sight. If it appears they are going to bungle it, move in and clean up."

The thin man, Farben, needed no further instructions. He knew what "clean up" meant. Fat Chen, an appellation the small man never used except within his own thoughts, had given such orders before. If the Neil Road team blew it, it was his job to kill them and their quarry. The bodies would never be found. That had been Chen's way from the time he had first appeared in Singapore twenty years earlier, weighing a mere two hundred pounds, filled with a burning ambition to be the richest man in the Far East. It was still his way and always would be. No loose ends. No leads back to him.

The two agents sat on separate cots in a cell, isolated from the other prisoners in the dank sub-basement of the Justice Building. One was of middle height, well muscled, his face squared off like a block of granite chiseled to form facial features. The other was the exact opposite, slim, wiry, the smooth face almost boyish.

"I can't remember ever being so stupid," the young-looking one said. "We walked right into it. We've had assignments like this before and never came close to blowing it. What the hell happened?"

"Don't know," Muscles answered, his elbows on his knees, his hands holding his head dejectedly. "It's as if they'd had a camera on our operation from the first. I feel like we've been orchestrated, you know? We didn't even have a chance to report back to Bangkok. They won't have a clue what happened to us."

"Well, in a couple of weeks it won't matter. The judge made that clear enough. Drug convictions carry the death penalty here. That's it."

"Did you understand all of it?" Muscles asked. "I'm not sure our lawyer translated it the way it went down. He made it sound too damn simple. They found a kilo of heroin in our car. They couldn't connect us to any drug ring."

"Didn't matter," the other agent, who sat cross-legged on the cot like a small Buddha, replied. "Possession was enough. They've got some kind of law here like the new 'zero tolerance' law being used back home. You're found with the stuff, you're guilty. Having some in our car was as bad as if we'd been peddling the stuff for years."

"You know what makes me feel worst?" Muscles said. "It was being taken so easily, led into a trap like a couple of rookies, drugged and left in the car."

"Chen's people. How did they get us to Kuala Lumpur, do you suppose?"

"In the back seat of our own car, I imagine. They just drove up here and left us in the front seat. Called the local police. It doesn't take a genius to figure it out."

"Did the judge say 'hanged by the neck'?"

"That's what the little bastard said," Muscles responded, the cords of his neck standing out as his venom spilled out. "He was a cold one. No extenuating circumstances. I wonder what he'd have done if it had happened to his son or a brother."

The boyish one sat, small hands folded, head bent as if in supplication. The AXE agent blinked rapidly, as if on the brink of tears. "So it's over." The words were barely audible, the voice full of emotion, almost choking. "I've been all over the world for Hawk, done every kind of job that he asked short of killing. And this is where it ends."

"Jesus! That's all I need," Muscles said, disgusted. "Don't be so goddamned maudlin. Let's spend our time figuring out how the hell to get out of here. I don't want to die in some fuckin' Malaysian prison at the end of a rope!"

"Face it, Barney. Hawk doesn't know where we are. What've we got? Two weeks? Less? No one knows where we are."

"But he'll make a try at it. No one abducts Hawk's agents without paying. Someday, some way, Hawk'll figure it out."

"Let's hope he figures it out in the next few days." The dejected agent formed the words without expression. "I don't want to die."

The big man had worn the miniature camera not because he was intelligent or talented. In fact he was just the opposite. Farben, his narrow-faced boss, moved around too much, checking his back, watching his surroundings. But when you told the big man to watch someone, he watched, immobile, like a rock.

Chen sat in his electronic room and saw his people carry the two agents out to their own car and plant the heroin in the trunk. He'd watched now and then as they left Singapore across the Johor Causeway and drove the two hundred miles into the middle of the peninsula, passing through the towns of Segamat and Seremban en route to the big city, Kuala Lumpur.

Farben's partner sat in the courtroom, detached, as the camera hidden in his clothes ground on, telling the whole story. Chen had been confident of the outcome. The Malaysians had tunnel vision as far as drugs were concerned. If you wanted to commit murder in Malaysia today, all you had to do was plant some drugs on your intended victim, call the police, and sit back. Bureaucracy took care of the rest.

Fat Chen switched off when the sentence had been passed and the two were led away. It was a closed issue and he had other fish to fry.

TWO

The woman raised herself on one elbow and looked down at the dark-haired man beside her. They were both naked. Before they had gone to bed, he had turned the air conditioning off and opened the sliding doors to the night air. The moonlight reflected off the Gulf of Mexico into the room.

She looked at him for long minutes as if she couldn't get enough of him. He seemed taller than his six-feet-one frame as he stretched out beside her. His face in repose seemed softer when he was asleep. Awake, the strong features came alive with vitality and the dark eyes looked at her, sometimes with intensity, sometimes with laughter, all crinkled at the edges.

His body was tanned, but the collection of scars he'd picked up over the years showed through, slightly less brown, shiny in some places, slightly puckered in others. She had not asked him about them. She guessed he'd been a soldier, perhaps a mercenary, but that didn't fit the pattern of their few days together. He dressed well, looked better than most men in a tuxedo, played cards with her men friends with an expertise she'd seldom seen, and fascinated her female friends with a knowledge of subjects that seemed endless.

They'd made love often and the ecstasy she'd felt seemed to grow with each encounter. He was an expert lover. He seemed to know all the right places to touch her, and knew how to bring her along at a pace that maximized her pleasure. Then, as if his instincts were perfect, he knew when to take her to the peak of passion and hold her there for long minutes while she felt sensations rush through her she had never felt before.

It was the kind of treatment that made slaves of women. She knew that. But she also realized that he was the kind of man she couldn't keep with her much longer. Still, she had to try, to travel with him to the heights as many times as possible before he left her. And when he did leave, she would follow if it were at all possible.

Eloise Harper was an individual of many talents. She was the only woman who had been acceptted into the closed society of the frontons. Jai alai was her game. She'd played it as hard as any man and was rated as one of the best. Her father, a Longboat Key real estate developer who could afford to indulge her every whim, built a structure resembling a jai alai fronton for her next to the tennis courts on their estate on Florida's Gulf Coast. It was constructed of cement, rectangular, open on one side and with no roof. It seemed to be half again as long as a tennis court.

Nick Carter had been a natural pupil. In the few days he had been with her, she had fitted him with a cesta, the player's catching and throwing basket. It was strapped to his right arm and extended in a graceful curve, like an oversize bread basket shaped like a quarter moon. It extended about thirty inches beyond his wrist. She taught him many of the complicated moves of the best players. The skills he quickly developed seemed to center around accuracy and pace. He could place the small rock-hard ball anywhere he wanted and with the exact speed to either blow past his opponent or set her up with a soft shot. The long, curved basket strapped to his right arm seemed a part of him already. Given time, she knew she could make him one of the best.

Carter opened his eyes. The woman's face was close to his, her long blond hair sweeping across his torso, her breath a whisper of air that moved the hair on his chest.

She was lovely, her body perfect, her breasts jutting and proud, her legs long and muscular without detracting from her femininity. She was strong, stronger than most women he met, but it was not evident until she needed the strength to challenge him in bed or on the fronton court.

The hazel eyes looked into his and the message was plain. She was insatiable. He didn't know how long he'd slept, but she was ready for him again. He felt relaxed for the first time in weeks, able to close his eyes and let sleep take him without fear of an enemy attack. It was exactly what he'd needed.

He raised his head and kissed her softly on the lips. "Relax," he said, reaching to the night table for his cigarettes. He flipped two from the pack, lit them with his gold lighter, and slipped one between her lips. "We should have plenty of time."

He knew the statement was more of a vain hope than a certainty. He could be called at any moment and their brief

encounter would be over. No sooner had the thought occurred . . .

"Don't answer it," she said, as the phone rang insis-
tently. She seemed to sense, as he did, that it was the signal
for parting.

Carter reached for the receiver and recognized the simu-
lated voice of the computer that Hawk had installed a couple of years earlier. Recently some clown at the agency had
programmed the damned thing to track him down and pass
along orders. He'd have preferred the warm voice of
Ginger Bateman, David Hawk's right hand, even if her
calls usually took him away from pleasure to the games of
silent war that his agency fought.

"Nick Carter, please," the synthesized voice said.

"What do you want?"

"We have need of your presence," the complicated as-
sembly of chips and wires communicated.

"Where is he?"

"In his office. The message seemed urgent."

Carter hung up. He didn't feel the need to say good-bye
to a machine. He sometimes wondered if he had been in
the business too long. More and more, in the assignments
Hawk gave him, he encountered computer-controlled bar-
riers. He was flesh and blood. He depended on his wits,
his knife, and his gun to get the job done. He was skilled in
the use of most modern weapons and could fly almost any
aircraft to a reasonable level of skill, but he was weary of
the opposition gearing up with state-of-the-art electronics
to run their operations. More and more, he wondered if one
of the computers, particularly after artificial intelligence
was perfected, would be the death of him.

"Who was that?" Eloise asked, crushing out her cigarette and coming to him, holding him close.

"You wouldn't believe me if I told you."

"Try me."

He smiled to himself at the two words, having tried her many times in the past few days. "A computer."

"You're putting me on."

"I wish I were. When my work calls, they sometimes turn a computer loose to find me. It's like getting in an elevator and hearing a mechanical voice telling you what to do, how to move, when to get off," he said, taking the last drag of his cigarette and reaching for her. "I hate it."

"Well, you don't have to go this very minute," she whispered, covering his mouth with hers. She pressed against him from chest to toe, willing him to take her one more time, to leave with her a final memory that would be indelible.

When she let him up for air, he chuckled. "Let the damned computer wait."

When he pulled her beneath him and entered her, his passion mounting, the phone rang again.

Viciously, he swept up the receiver and before he could answer, the electronic voice announced: "I have an Eastern flight out of Sarasota in one hour that connects with Delta in Atlanta for Washington with only a forty-minute layover. The tickets are at the Eastern counter in the name of Jack Clifford."

The connection was broken as he smashed down the receiver.

The Delta flight took him into Washington's National Airport. Carter took a cab to his brownstone in George-town, showered, packed a suitcase with fresh clothes, and drove his beautifully restored Jaguar XKE across the Theodore Roosevelt Bridge and up New Hampshire Avenue to

Dupont Circle. He drove around the circle, past AXE headquarters in the Amalgamated Press and Wire Services building, to a small side street a couple of blocks to the north. Miraculously, he found a parking spot in the congested neighborhood.

Amalgamated Press and Wire Services was the front for a highly secret intelligence agency, AXE, run by David Hawk, his boss, probably the keenest mind in the Western intelligence community. But that fact was known by very few people. Hawk had been one of the best fieldmen for years before he took to his desk. It was reputed that he'd been with "Wild Bill" Donovan, the founder of the OSS, the forerunner of the Central Intelligence Agency. Carter had never brought the subject up. Hawk would have to have been a very young man if the rumor was true and a lot older now than he looked.

AXE had been formed at the request of the president after too many leaks in the other clandestine services had caused too many unnecessary deaths. Hawk was a friend and the most logical man to be given the task. Carter was Hawk's best agent, but there was more to their relationship than mere professional respect. While the older man's manner was brusque and commanding, his feelings for Carter were almost fatherly, although he rarely allowed overt expressions of concern to surface.

The walk back to Dupont Circle was a ritual with Carter. He never approached directly any location where he was expected. He had too many enemies. Too many operatives in rival agencies knew him by sight. So it was his caution, an obsession with him, that kept him alive when others he had known were long dead.

This time his sharply honed senses told him he was being observed. He walked around Dupont Circle on the west side without looking directly at AXE headquarters. He stopped frequently, once to light a cigarette, once to tie a shoe, and his eyes covered the ground all around him without seeing anything out of place. Still it was there— the feeling persisted.

Instead of going to the Amalgamated Press offices, Carter stepped into a phone booth and called Hawk's private number.

"Yes," the gruff voice barked at the mouthpiece.

Carter could imagine his boss sitting in the high-backed swivel chair, a foul-smelling cigar in his mouth, smoke circling to the ceiling. Hawk was of middle height, stocky, and usually wore dark blue or gray suits. He had a full head of startlingly white hair.

"Carter," he announced. "I'm at a pay phone near the circle. I think I'm being followed."

"Lose them. Meet me at the safe house on Vermont Avenue."

Carter hailed a cab and asked the driver to take him to the Federal Bureau of Investigation. He flipped a twenty beside the driver a block before they arrived and was out of the taxi and into the FBI monolith before anyone following could react.

He knew the ground floor well. He took a back entrance, hailed another cab, and was heading back northwest again in seconds. He slipped out of the cab at the Washington Plaza Hotel, entered the lobby, and headed for the side door and another taxi stand. By the time he stood a block away from the safe house, he knew he had lost his pursuer.

The old brownstone on Vermont Avenue was in the middle of the block, one of several refurbished in a block community project. A couple, low-level agents of AXE, fronted the house for Hawk, attended local community meetings, shopped, cut the grass, and looked like any other retired couple.

Hawk was in the second-floor-front sanctuary he sometimes used when he wanted to get away from the demands of his office. He stood at the front window, his mouth pulling on the inevitable foul cigar, his hands clasped behind his back. He turned when Carter entered.

"Who was on you?" he demanded impatiently. Never a man with an abundance of tolerance for interruptions to his plans, his attitude was almost hostile.

"I don't know, sir. I lost them."

"Sit down. I'd like you on a plane to Singapore as soon as possible. We've got a lot to cover."

Carter looked across a glass table at the older man. By keeping up with world news, he frequently was able to guess why he was being summoned. Totally relaxed in Florida, he hadn't opened a single copy of the *Sarasota Herald Tribune* that had been delivered to his room every day for more than a week.

"Two of our agents are missing in Singapore. One of our junior people in the area sent back word that they've been taken by the Malaysian authorities for drug possession. Apparently a kilo of heroin was found in their car. They're in a jail in Kuala Lumpur."

"Who set them up?"

"I don't know. I want them out of there. Drug possession is a hanging offense in Malaysia."

"Can't you use your contacts?"

"Not this time. The local people are adamant. Something like our zero tolerance policy on drugs. They make no exceptions."

"A little out of my line, isn't it?" Carter asked, taking a cigarette from a gold case and tapping the end before he lit it.

"On the surface, maybe," Hawk said, blowing smoke to the ceiling and getting up to pace in front of the window. "There's a lot going on in Singapore right now. Two CIA agents disappeared while working on the kidnapping of the Soo brothers. We sent in two of our people to find out what happened to them and they end up being framed. Stupid!"

"Aren't the Soos the brothers who were the snake oil kings of the Far East?" Carter asked.

"They started with Ginseng Essence Balm and built it into a conglomerate. Billionaires. Someone—some group we haven't identified—has taken them."

"But they're from Singapore. Our people are in Kuala Lumpur."

"I want you to find out what the hell's going on over there. The prime minister of Singapore is about to retire. Our information on his probable successor is not encouraging—the man has marked Soviet leanings."

"The prime minister's been in power since the sixties. He changed the place from an impoverished colony to an economic miracle, one of the trading leaders of the Far East," Carter mused. "He created an almost perfect society."

"Maybe too perfect. You know the place as well as I do. Squeaky clean. Fines for dropping a candy wrapper on the streets. Banners on almost every block extolling the value of work and thrift. Everyone is a money-crazed stock market fanatic. The children all wear uniforms to school and act like well-trained robots."

"It could be worse. It may seem artificial to us, but it's

better than guns everywhere, neighborhoods held hostage to crack, and homeless sleeping on the sidewalks."

"Could be," Hawk said, continuing to pace. He seemed to have boundless energy and had to work it off. "But the prime minister—what's his name?—Peter Hue Yen—has too many enemies. It's a valuable pie and one hell of a lot of people want a piece of it."

"Have you set up a cover?"

"No. Fly in as soon as possible. Go first class all the way. Stay at the Shangri-la, play the tables, nose around. Ginger has already made your reservations."

"What about our people in Kuala Lumpur?"

"You'll have to be in two places at the same time, Nick," Hawk said. "Maintain the rich tourist cover but get our people out of jail. Don't let anyone connect the two roles."

"And nose around to find out who took the Soo brothers and why," Carter finished for him. "Take a good look at the prime minister's successor. Find out who is backing him and his intent—"

"And if it goes against our interests, put a stop sign on it," Hawk interrupted.

"That it?"

"No. I've had word that someone in Singapore with incredible power may be pulling strings that affect your assignment."

"What do you know about him?"

"Not as much as I'd like. He's very powerful and very private. I've got a feeling you'll learn more from our people when you get them out."

"What do you want me to do with them? Send them home? Use them to help?"

"They could be a problem for you. Use your judgment. If you can't use them, send them to the Bangkok chief of station. I'll talk to him. He'll reassign them. If you want local help, call on him."

"Joe Wright still our man?"

"He's still there."

"Is Howard in town?"

Howard Schmidt was AXE's man of all trades—archivist, identifications chief, master of electronic gadgets. "He's in his basement lair as usual. You can get him through the computer."

"I've been meaning to speak to you about that computer—" Carter started to say.

"No changes to the computer," Hawk cut him off, raising one hand like a stop signal. The computer was a sensitive issue they had discussed before. "You've got to go with the times, Nick. We're programming it to do more every day."

Carter mumbled something under his breath. Hawk caught the word "progress" and some profanity. He almost cracked a smile.

"Forget about the computer, Nick," the older man said as Carter rose to leave. "Some things you just have to live with."

Back at his car, Carter sensed he was being watched again. It didn't really matter now. He was on his own, a condition that was second nature to him. He'd been operating alone for so long it might not be natural to feel safe and secure all the time. The vacations, like the one he'd had with Eloise, had been great, just what he needed between demanding jobs, but the action was the thing. He had an

assignment, one that was open-ended, and that had the po-
tential to take him in almost any direction.

So he had to forget about the Eloises of this world and
concentrate on the job at hand. The first thing he had to do
was find out who had him under surveillance.

THREE

Pan American flight 1 took Carter from New York to Los Angeles, to Hawaii, and finally to Hong Kong. With only an hour in Hong Kong, he boarded Singapore Airlines flight 146 for the remaining leg of the journey. The service on both flights had been luxurious, the crisp efficiency of the American flight attendants in sharp contrast to the fluid movements of the Malaysian crew who wore colorful long gowns in native batiks, their concern total for the comfort of the people in their charge.

But something had nagged at Carter. The short hairs at the back of his neck wouldn't permit him to fully relax during the flight. And it wasn't just the usual signals he was getting. They seemed to be coming from all directions, as if he had enemies everywhere.

The taxi driver at Changi Airport in Singapore tossed Carter's bag in the back of the cab and held the door for him.

"The American embassy," the man from AXE announced.

His last contact at AXE headquarters had been Howard Schmidt. The big man had pressed a new set of toys on him, or he'd tried. He'd designed an attaché case that held not only Carter's three favorite weapons, but a small leather case of syringes and drugs. This trip, Schmidt had included some new items.

"This cylinder contains a nerve gas," Schmidt had explained. "Released in an air duct, it will fill a building the size of our headquarters in seconds. No aftereffects, just a couple of hours of sleep and a mild headache."

"You know I like to travel light, Howard," Carter said, remembering the countless times he'd been through something like this with the gadgets man. "You'll have to send this by diplomatic courier. I'll just have to find a place to conceal them when I get there."

"They could be helpful. What about the Soo kidnapping? The gas could be useful in neutralizing their enemies."

"You've been reading too many spy novels, Howard. What are all these things, the balls? They look like grenades," Carter asked, hefting one of the plum-sized metal balls in one hand. "Are you turning me into a mercenary?"

"You don't have to use them. Just something new. Four times the power of a regulation grenade. They're equipped with timers you can set quickly, from five to twenty seconds. The pins pull out more easily than those of conventional grenades. But you've got to be careful with these babies. Each one is capable of blowing up a small building or totally demolishing a car."

"Leave the gas in the case, but I'll be damned if I'm going to carry around a bunch of those things."

"Aw, Nick—"

"Just take them out. I'm not declaring war on anyone."
He had to humor his friend Howard once in a while, but
the compromise was the best he was about to make. The
big man spent too much time alone in the confines of his
basement kingdom dreaming up weird contraptions for
AXE agents to use. He knew that Carter wouldn't use
some of his truly outlandish inventions and Carter had
never talked to the other agents about them.

Now in the "Lion City," the taxi driver, a small, chain-
smoking native, drove sedately, unlike his peers. He
cruised along the East Coast Parkway pointing out the
Swimming Center, the Tennis Center, the golf driving
range, the Big Splash, a winding tubular affair populated
by hundreds of kids sliding down the tubes amid a rush of
white water. His voice was melodious, a singsong of
sound, but his English was almost impossible to follow.

Carter was getting the full tourist treatment. At that
point in time, he didn't really care. He'd probably get the
full tour of Chinatown before they headed for Hill Street
and the embassy.

Carter was familiar with Singapore, as he was with most
major cities in the world. They passed the beautiful Arme-
nian Church before pulling up in front of the embassy. In
bright sunlight, the church was as white as a newly white-
washed fence. It looked like a typical New England village
church. The fact that they'd passed it confirmed that he'd
been taken for a "tourist ride." The church was at Coleman
and Hill streets. They should have come in from the north,
past Stamford Road, not from the south.

It took him no more than five minutes at the embassy to
retrieve Howard's case, but not before he'd received the
usual warnings from the ambassador's chargé d'affaires.

Why were the desk jockeys all so damn pompous? Why did they all feel obliged to tell him to keep out of trouble? He had a job to do and they knew it. Bureaucrats. He could survive quite well without them.

Back in the cab, he spoke to the driver in Mandarin, knowing it was probably the man's native tongue. "The Shangri-la Hotel. Take Stamford Road, Orchard Road, and Orange Grove Road. No detours this time. I don't feel like another tour, old father."

As they circled to the right up the incline of Orange Grove Road, the Shangri-la loomed at them out of the trees. He'd been there before and knew it well, one of the ten highest-rated hotels in the world.

His suite was magnificent, three rooms with every luxury and convenience a man could desire. His balcony, one of a hundred in an annex building, seemed like part of a giant staircase leading down to the pool area. The whole series of balconies was covered with clinging vines, all in bloom, their fragrance almost overpowering, their orange, red, and yellow blossoms adding to the incredible beauty of the place.

To his right, a man-made fountain flowed noisily down a hundred-foot drop to the side of a poolside restaurant that was well placed between the luxury annex and the towering main building. In the near distance, the lush grass of a golf course on the grounds added to the view.

But Carter hadn't come here for play. He flipped open the attaché case, withdrew Wilhelmina, his 9mm Luger, and strapped the holster on so she rested under his left armpit. Hugo, his needle-sharp stiletto, he strapped to his right forearm under his jacket. Sitting loosely in its chamois sheath, he could easily flip it into the palm of his hand with the simple flick of his wrist. The weapons were familiar. With them he felt complete. They had saved his life more times than he could count. When he'd been younger and less jaded, he'd named them as he might old friends and the names had stuck.

He had one more familiar weapon, a small gas bomb the size of a large walnut that he wore taped to his inner thigh when on assignment. He called the bomb Pierre. He could reach for it in an emergency, twist the two halves, and, holding his breath, render others in the same room unconscious. Sometimes Pierre contained lethal gas. This Pierre, the last of many he'd left behind in life and death situations, was lethal. The case also contained the cylinder of nerve gas Schmidt had pressed on him in Washington.

The last item he brought out was a black leather case small enough to fit into a pocket. It held a half-dozen miniature syringes and three vials of liquid, all of different colors. The green liquid rendered a victim unconscious. The orange liquid was a truth serum. The red was lethal. A few drops of any of the three were highly effective. Carter had used them in the past and found the assortment to be extremely helpful in a variety of situations.

He opened a closet and was about to toss the attaché case on a shelf when he stopped, totally surprised. A jai alai cesta was on the shelf. He took it down and examined it. It was the one Eloise had loaned him in Florida. No note was attached, but none was necessary. With the discovery, a lot of things were falling into place.

It was her way of saying she wanted to be with him. It explained the eyes on him in Washington and all the way to Singapore. If you had enough money you could buy men who could find out anything for you, could track anyone without detection. The problem was real. If she was just trying to be with him, that was one thing. If she'd been a plant from a foreign agency all along, that was another.

Carter searched the room as thoroughly as he could without the assistance of electronic gadgetry. He found two listening devices. The screws holding the huge mirror in the bathroom had been tampered with recently. He was probably looking at a one-way mirror. It was obvious that he was under intense scrutiny. Was it the caprice of a smitten woman, or something else? Either way he didn't like it.

Carter's suite was at the end of the hall next to the waterfall. He walked silently to the door of the neighboring suite, swiftly picked the lock, and moved into the sun-drenched quarters with Wilhelmina in his right hand.

A man was sitting at a desk, unsuspecting, earphones clamped to his head.

Carter placed the cold muzzle of his Luger behind the man's ear. "Don't make any stupid moves," he said. "Take off the earphones, put your hands in the air, and turn around slowly."

The man was dressed in a Brooks Brothers suit, his tie expensive, his shoes custom-made. He was clean-cut, not too different in appearance from the average FBI man, but with more expensive tastes. He appeared to be American. "Who are you?" Carter snapped.

"My pocket?" the man asked, pointing.

Carter nodded.

The man reached into an inner pocket carefully and brought out his wallet. He flipped it open. The card was embossed in gold. The man's picture, in color, took up half the space.

TAMPA CONFIDENTIAL
Jeff Bridgetown

"Get your hands in the air," Carter ordered. "You're a long way from Tampa, Bridgetown. Did Eloise Harper send you?"

"I don't reveal the identity of my clients."

"You don't have any idea what you're dealing with," Carter said menacingly. "If Eloise is being foolish, trying to stretch out something that's over, that's one thing and no threat to me. But if our meeting was planned and she's not what she seems, then you could end up very stiff and cold a long way from home." While he spoke, he flipped Hugo into his palm, held the point just below the man's right ear, and holstered his gun.

Bridgetown was quiet for a moment or two. Carter traced a thin line with Hugo from Bridgetown's ear to his throat. Small drops of blood ran to the edge of the man's collar. The two were almost nose to nose. "What will it be?" Carter demanded. "Are you willing to die for a woman with an overactive libido?"

"I sometimes work for her father," the man said calmly. "She called me."

"What for?"

"To keep track of you, to find out who you really are and what you do."

"You didn't get this far alone. No one is that good."

"No. I've got a team."

"Too bad you didn't cover your back," Carter said. "Where are they?"

Bridgetown glanced at a walkie-talkie next to him. "I can call them. They'd be here in seconds."

"Never mind," Carter said, slipping Hugo back into its sheath. He was satisfied that the team was harmless, that Eloise was just a woman with too much money and a father who was too indulgent. "I'm just going to say this once. You're in way over your head. You might be good, but you're a dead man if you don't pack up and go home. You and your team."

"She told me about the scars on your body. I figured you weren't your average citizen."

"So why didn't you advise her to leave me alone?"

"A buck's a buck. You don't get plum assignments like this every day," Bridgetown said, moving out of Carter's space and lowering his hands.

"Then consider it a vacation," Carter said. "You were very lucky, Bridgetown, you and your people."

"So what do I tell my client?"

"You'll think of something, I'm sure. Tell her to let me go and to look elsewhere for company. Make it stick. I don't want her mooning around here. She could end up dead." The expression on his face told the story. He was serious and no one could mistake the fact.

"I'll do that," Bridgetown said. "We're out of here. Okay?"

"Make it fast. I've got work to do," Carter said. "Eloise is spoiled. She made a bad mistake."

"I was beginning to think the same thing," Bridgetown said. "You're more than a businessman or a tourist, Carter. No one's ever taken me like this."

"What's your background?"

"CIA. Too much conflict in the Company. It's better to work for yourself."

"You've seen enough to know you'd better pack up?" Carter asked, buying the man's story.

"You bet. What are you, Carter? Some kind of super-spook?"

"You know better than to ask," Carter said. "When you report back, make damn sure she gets a very bland picture of me. If she gets in the way . . . well."

"I get the message."

Carter made him assume the position and relieved him of a .357 magnum. "Why so much firepower?" he asked.

"Some of my work gets too close to the bone."

"I'll hang on to this. Just clear out and get the message across. It's in your best interests. If you don't, you'll have more than you can handle."

"Whatever. You want me to take back the jai alai thing-umajig?"

Carter pushed the private investigator to the door. "No. Just make a fast exit and don't look back," he said. "Again, think of it as a short exotic vacation."

When he'd gone, Carter coded a series of numbers into one of the phones he'd checked for bugs in his own suite. He was annoyed that Eloise would be so stupid, so self-centered. It meant he'd have to check on her, make sure she was just a foolish, overly romantic woman and not a threat.

Hawk was not in. He spoke to Ginger, and told her to have someone check out Eloise Harper. He hung up and gave all his attention to the job at hand. He'd wasted enough time on nonessentials.

He called the desk and asked them to order a rental car, something powerful but plain, preferably black. Kuala Lumpur was obviously the first point of attack, but he wanted to make some impression in Singapore first.

Carter dressed in a lightweight safari suit, short-sleeved, and headed for the counter. He picked up the keys to the rental and headed for the docks. No one followed. He sat at an open-air bar next to the dock where tourists were lined up for a tour of the harbor in an old Chinese junk with red sails. While they boarded, he watched the people around him. No one seemed suspicious. No one was interested in his movements . . . as far as he could tell.

So much for establishing his base. He returned to the room and prepared for the trip inland. He packed a small bag that contained an outfit all in black—jumpsuit, sneakers, and stevedore cap—and as an afterthought, tossed in the cylinder Schmidt had sent along.

The Justice Building in Kuala Lumpur was in the middle of the city, in an old section, surrounded by other old red brick buildings. It was three stories high. Carter sat in the rental in his black outfit. He had kept clear of the few streetlights, changed from his safari suit in the car, and blackened his face. His familiar weapons were in place.

Before heading for the old building, he had eaten his evening meal in a café run by an aged Chinese. The man had been attracted to an American who could speak his tongue.

"What brings you to our city, younger brother?" the ancient gentleman asked, keeping his eyes on his help while he rested his tired feet.

"I'm an architect back home. I spend my vacations looking at old buildings."

"We have many old buildings. What do you want to see?" the old man asked. He was small, very thin, but very bright. Nothing escaped him. He knew what was happening in every corner of his establishment while talking to the stranger.

"I design penal institutions back home."

The old man rolled his tongue around the literal translation. "I know not the word."

"Prisons. I design jails."

"Ah. We have many jails. Much theft. Too much dope trading. Bad. Very bad."

Carter smiled to himself at the hypocrisy. The old man was an opium user himself. He had all the signs. He even smelled of the last pipe he'd smoked. "I hear that drug smuggling is a hanging offense."

The old man was wary. As a user, he could be pulled in and sent to the scaffold. His only safety lay in the number of his people who were as addicted as he. The police could not take them all, so they left the users and went after the dealers. "You have heard right, younger brother," he finally said. "You look more like a policeman than an architect. How do I know you are not trying to trap an old man?"

"I have no traps, older brother. I simply observe. Where is the jail they keep the condemned?" He tossed in the question casually.

"Not many condemned right now. The dealers are lying low. If anyone is awaiting the hangman, he will be in the Justice Building." The old man smiled for the first time, revealing teeth blackened by the smoke of many pipes. They were mostly stumps, most uneven, some missing. The parchment skin of his face wrinkled as he went on. "Poor devils. What are they to do? We have used the powder and paste for hundreds of years. Smugglers are fourth and fifth generation. Are they to become fishermen or panderers?"

"I hear even foreigners are condemned to death," Carter added as he finished off the last of his coffee.

"I am told that two are in the basement cells of the

Justice Building now," the old man said. He suddenly looked weary. A frown creased his ancient face. "But you will excuse me. Business is a tireless master."

That had been a couple of hours earlier. Carter had been watching the building since then. Police cars had brought in prisoners. He had seen no one leave who was not in uniform. It was late, too late for court appearances and the work of lawyers.

Carter had mulled over the situation carefully. He couldn't go in blasting. The operation had to be as clean as he could make it. Howard Schmidt's latest invention rested on the seat beside him. The nerve gas was obviously the answer, but it, too, presented problems. He could hold his breath longer than most people, at least four minutes. That was all right for him, but what about the prisoners? How big were they? Could he carry them both out? He decided on a soft probe first.

Carter circled the building quietly. Fortunately, it stood alone with an empty lot between it and its neighbors on both sides. The weed-covered lots were being prepared for an expansion to the old building.

A small parking lot at the back held only three cars. A dim bulb shone over a small door, the only opening at the rear. Carter opened it a crack and peered down the length of a deserted hall.

With the agility of a night-stalking creature, he slipped inside and descended to the first basement, taking the narrow stairway two steps at a time.

"What are you doing . . . ?" a voice behind him started to say.

Carter swung without hesitation and chopped the lone guard on the side of the neck. The man went down hard. Carter dragged him to a door nearby and shoved him in among the brooms and mops. A mobile laundry hamper took up the rest of the space.

Carter found no cells on that floor, but he did find a small elevator at the end of the hall. There was no way he was going to use the elevator now, but it might be useful later.

He took the stairs to the next lower level, making a mental note of every detail as he went, including the venting system.

The second basement contained a group of small storage offices, a closet identical to the one on the floor above, and one long row of cells. A guard was watching television, his back to Carter.

The Killmaster crept up slowly, his black sneakers making no noise on the painted cement floor. He grasped the guard in a choke hold and held him immobile. Since most of the population was Chinese, he whispered in the man's ear in Mandarin, "Where are the two Americans?"

"I don't . . . understand," the man choked out in Cantonese.

Carter repeated the question in the guard's language.

"They are in the last cell to the right. They—" he started to say as Carter cut him off, rendering him unconscious.

The man from AXE deposited the unconscious guard in the closet directly below the one he'd used upstairs. The guard had no keys. Despite the decrepit appearance of the jail, all doors were controlled electronically from a control room.

He ran along the hall to the last cell. "Where is the control room?" he asked the two dejected Americans without preliminaries.

He must have looked like an apparition. "Hawk sent

me," he hissed at them. "You know the layout of this place?"

"Part of the job," the smaller of the two said.

"Where the hell's the control room for the cell doors?"

"Main floor. Second door to the right."

"I'm going to take you out. Stay as close to the cell door as you can," Carter said, taking off at a run, not waiting for an answer. There was no point in telling them he might have to use the gas. He had the lay of the land now. He could handle it.

The two flights of stairs to the back door were scaled in seconds. He slipped around to the front, keeping to the shadows.

The cylinder would be useful after all. He took it from the car and clipped it to his belt. He unraveled a long thin wire from around his waist and attached a grappling hook that he unfolded from a pocketknife that resembled a Swedish army knife.

It took him two attempts and more noise than he intended before the small grappling hook caught and held. He donned gloves and pulled himself up the wire, hand over hand.

The roof was flat. A relatively modern rooftop air conditioner hummed quietly to one side. One of the two large fans alongside the unit was circulating air down below.

The simplest task was releasing the gas and leaving the cylinder propped up beside the air intake. The more difficult one was to get in and then escape detection while transporting two inert bodies.

Carter decided not to waste time trying to find a way in from the roof. He rappelled down the side of the building in seconds and was at the front door ready to move in when two officers entered in front of him, reporting for duty.

Too many variables, he said to himself. He hadn't checked on the time factors for the nerve gas. Schmidt said it would last for several hours, but how long would it take for it to take effect? He couldn't allow for people entering the building. His best bet was to get in fast, then use the elevator and the back door on his way out. He took two minutes to move his car to the rear parking lot, then glided, catlike, around to the front door.

No one was in sight. Carter took in several lungsful of air, expelling each, building up a high concentration of oxygen in his blood. Through long practice and the use of yoga techniques, he was capable of holding his breath for four minutes. Once, trapped in a submarine, fighting for his life, he had extended his limit to five minutes but had blacked out at that point. There was no way he could allow himself to black out today.

Carter crept in past the brightly lit front entrance and down the hall to the control room. On the way he passed the two officers he'd seen enter. They had made it only a few feet inside the door. He didn't stop. Every fraction of a second was precious.

Two men were slumped over the control panel. The panel's instructions were in German. The guards had duplicated them using Chinese characters. German was no problem for the Killmaster. He pulled the guards aside and found a switch that controlled the cells in the second basement and threw it. He left one of the guard's bodies drooped over it.

He took the elevator to the second basement. It was painfully slow. He checked his Rolex. A minute and a half had passed already. The door slid open to reveal two more guards on the floor, one toppled over on the other. Carter found the closet where he'd left the guard earlier, pulled out the laundry basket, a canvas affair with a metal frame over four sturdy casters, and wheeled it down the hall to the last cell.

Two and a half minutes.

As he worked, he thought the agents were an unlikely team, one so much smaller than the other, almost like a boy. He tossed the inert frame of the big man on the bottom and eased the smaller one on top of him. He covered them both with a soiled sheet, a precaution that was more prevention than necessity, and had them to the elevator before the third minute was up.

The elevator crawled to the main floor slowly. Carter was beginning to feel uncomfortable, small black and green spots floating before his eyes from time to time.

At last the elevator opened on the main floor. He pushed the cart toward the rear of the building, the casters playing tricks with him, the cart bouncing off the walls, first one side, then the other.

He came to the end of the hall and found a hallway crossing like a T. Which way? He turned left and soon found himself trapped at a dead end. Three times he had to stop and shove bodies out of the way.

Carter reversed his path and took the other end of the T. Aftster twenty feet it turned sharply to the right and he was faced with a set of double doors. They were locked. He whipped out his Luger and shattered the lock. It took three rounds before the door gave way to a powerful kick from his right foot.

Four and a half minutes.

Carter was feeling the pressure build, threatening to pop his ears if he didn't release it. He exhaled, careful not to take in any of the gas. His vision was blurred and his actions slowed.

He reached the door and pushed the cart out into the night air just as his knees stared to buckle. As the door closed behind them, he took a long breath, drawing the fresh air deep within his lungs.

He still wasn't out of danger. He struggled to his feet on rubbery knees and pushed the cart to his car. He opened the car door, threw aside the sheet, and lifed out the first AXE agent.

He had just placed the smaller body on the back seat when someone shouted from the other side of the lot. He grabbed for the other agent and had him half in the car when he felt two slugs tear into the flesh of his burden, followed by the sound of two shots.

Carter dropped the agent, whipped out his own gun, and crouched beside the car, offering as little target as possible.

Two officers appeared out of the darkness, their guns raised. The Killmaster dropped one with a leg shot. The other spun around and dropped, a 9mm bullet in one shoulder.

Carter kicked their guns to one side in the darkness as they lay moaning on the asphalt. He clubbed them senseless and left them to be found. There was no need to kill officers doing their duty, but he couldn't afford to be recognized or have them register the license of his car as he sped away.

The big agent was dead. Carter left him, with regrets, and scrambled into the car. Within seconds he was blocks from the Justice Building headed for the highway back to Singapore, two hundred miles away.

FOUR

In the rear parking lot, Carter changed to his street clothes. The special annex for the luxury suites offered the kind of privacy not available for patrons who had to enter through the lobby to get to their rooms.

A parking lot entrance permitted Carter to hoist the small agent on his shoulder and get up to the suite by way of the back stairs. In minutes he was in the suite, breathing hard, the agent on the floor at his feet, without anyone seeing them.

In the light of the luxury suite, the crumpled form at his feet looked more like a street beggar than one of AXE's best people. Hawk had said little about the team except for their value to him. They had been working the Far East for years with great success. It was a real coincidence that his path had not crossed with theirs before.

How long had it been since the gas took effect? Carter asked himself. About four hours. This one could be out for another hour yet. He really didn't know. Carter lifted the inert form and deposited the agent carefully in the spare bedroom. The stevedore cap the operative had been wearing slipped off revealing a head of closely cropped chestnut hair. The agent was filthy and Carter guessed probably infested with lice from the other inmates of the jail. The Killmaster decided to strip the body and get rid of the clothes.

Carter slipped off the agent's running shoes, unbuttoned and unzipped the dirt-encrusted jeans and pulled them off, tossing them on a sheet he'd laid out on the floor. The bare legs were dirty. They were well formed but not muscular. And they were hairless.

The jacket was easier to take off, and Carter threw it on top of the pants. The shirt was buttoned to the neck. He made short work of the buttons but stopped as he peeled the material back from the bare torso. Small rosebuds of breasts jutted from the chest. They were a mystery, either the fashion-model-sized breasts of a woman, or the drug-induced breasts of a man who preferred the role of a woman.

Carter was puzzled. Why dress and act as a man if you really wanted to be a woman? he wondered. Well, he could always try for the acid test. He peeled the boxer shorts from the inert form to reveal a flat, satin-smooth belly ending in a soft triangle that matched the chestnut hair of her head.

He cursed aloud. Carter was annoyed not only at himself for feeling like a voyeur, but at Hawk for not filling him in. There was no way this woman could have passed herself off as a man for years without Hawk knowing.

He looked down at the slim form and couldn't help an appraisal, even under the strange circumstances. This was a beautiful woman, boyishly slim, but somehow very desirable.

But she was in desperate need of a bath. He decided he might as well go the whole route. He peeled off the rest of the shirt and the grimy socks. He tossed them onto the sheet, tied it into a bundle, and left her on the bed while he ran a bath.

The bathroom was all black tiles, mirrors, smoked plastic partitions, and gold faucets. The tub was raised about twenty inches above the floor. To start the tub, Carter had to climb two carpeted stairs. The toilet and bidet were in separately partitioned sections of the room, but the divisions were of smoked plastic. One whole wall was mirrored.

He returned to the bedroom to find her curled up on one side. He slid his arms under her, feeling more paternal than anything else, and carried her into the luxurious bathroom. He made sure the water level was just enough to cover her, rested her head securely in a special sponge sling provided for the purpose, then headed for the living room and a phone.

Carter punched in a series of numbers that would give him entry into the AXE computer. He wasn't worried about the hotel switchboard. It had been installed originally as one of the first totally electronic services in the Far East. No one would be monitoring him.

"Nick. How is the job going?" the electronic voice asked.

His codes had given the computer instant recognition. Its circuits would know about his assignment and Hawk's whereabouts. While he had to admit it saved time, Carter still felt some resentment at the lack of human contact. He and Ginger Bateman had something going a long time ago and still had a strong bond between them. He missed the small asides and jibes that no whiz kid could build into the computer's memory banks.

"Just connect me with Hawk," he said.

"What is it, N3?" Hawk asked. He seemed to be preoccupied. The use of Carter's official designation said something about his mood.

"I lost one of our people," Carter reported. "I'm sorry. Maybe I could have avoided it. I wasn't in very good shape at the time."

"I'm sure you did your best, Nick," Hawk said, his tone now solicitous. "Who was it?"

"We didn't talk about names at my briefing. It was the big one."

"Barney. Damn! We can't afford to lose any agents. Let me rephrase that . . . I hate to lose any agent, a rookie or someone like Barney. Jesus! How's Sam?"

"Don't you mean Samantha?"

"Yes. What's your problem? I detect a note of belligerence there."

"I had to find out her sex a piece at a time. I brought her back to my hotel unconscious, and she was filthy from the jail. I thought she could use a delousing."

"And, I'm sure she'll express her appreciation at your concern for her well-being."

Carter sighed. "I just don't like that kind of shock, sir. Sorry about Barney. I didn't know him."

"A good man. He'll be missed. I'll get Joe Wright to claim the body. How did Sam take it?"

"I had to use Howard's new gas. She hasn't come out of it yet. I left her soaking in a tub. She'll probably be out for another hour. What's her full name? Tell me about her."

"Samantha Trail. Her partner was Barney Feldman. We

recruited her from the CIA, him from the Mossad."

"What about the Harper woman? I asked Ginger to check on her."

"Harmless. If you'd learn to keep your pants—"

"Let's not go into my private life," Carter interrupted his boss. "What about Sam? You want me to send her home or maybe to Joe Wright in Bangkok?"

"Keep her with you, Nick. She'll miss Barney. It'll be a hell of a shock," Hawk said. "She knows Singapore like the back of her hand and she's got an organization there. Keep her busy. You'll learn a lot about the place."

"I don't need a partner on this, particularly a grieving woman."

"*You bastard*!" a woman's voice screamed at him from the door.

"That her?" Hawk asked.

Carter turned to see her standing, dripping, a towel wrapped around her. "That's her. I'll talk to you later."

He hung up and moved toward her. She backed away.

"Don't you remember me? I pulled you out of the Justice Building."

"So where's Barney? He wouldn't leave me alone with someone like you."

"I was the one in black who told you I'd get you out. Barney didn't make it. I'm sorry."

"Barney . . . didn't . . ." Her hand went to her mouth and she gradually sank to her knees.

He went to her and scooped her up in his arms. As he carried her to the bed she flailed at him harmlessly and moaned her loss.

"Barney . . . Barney . . . I can't believe he's gone. How did it happen?"

Carter poured a brandy from a small flask he usually

carried. He held her head and made her slide most of it down her throat. She choked on it but got it down.

She smelled of the expensive soap provided by the hotel. Despite her surprise at finding herself in a strange tub, she must have taken time to soap herself. The towel had slipped down. She looked beautiful, vulnerable, and desirable all at the same time. Carter no longer felt paternal.

"I *know* you. I know who you are," she blurted out as the brandy glass slipped from her hand. She pulled up the towel and moved away from him. "You're Carter. You're *the* Nick Carter. Jesus! I don't know what to say."

Carter had experienced similar reactions before when confronted by new recruits, but never with a seasoned agent, and one who was probably the best in the Far East. He pulled back the sheet, fluffed up the pillow, and motioned her to slip between the sheets. He poured her another brandy, moved to the other side of the bed, and lit a cigarette.

"Can I have one, please?" she asked.

He gave her one, and she held it out to be lit. "You didn't answer my question." Her voice was low and her hand shook. It was obvious to Carter that she'd been through one of the worst ordeals of her career.

"I'm truly sorry about Barney. Hawk told me he was one hell of a guy," Carter started. "I had to feed a knockout gas into the ventilation system. I took you both out in a laundry hamper, Barney on the bottom. In the parking lot, I'd just dumped you in the back seat of my car and was hoisting Barney on my back when officers fired on us. They hit Barney," he went on, his voice expressionless. "I put them out of action and checked on Barney. He was gone. I got the hell out of there and brought you here."

She put the brandy glass on the night table, the cigarette in an ashtray, and started to sob uncontrollably, turning toward him, grabbing at another human being to help her through her pain.

"He was good, you know? He was...Oh, hell...he was a good guy, the best partner....We didn't have anything going...you know...nothing like that. But he was a *friend*. He saved my ass more than once. Jesus! I can't believe he's gone."

She clung to Carter until the sobs stopped. She wiped her eyes with the edge of the sheet, sat up against the back of the bed, holding the towel in one hand, and reached for her cigarette again. It had burned down. Carter lit another for her.

"Tell me about your case," he said, looking into the brown eyes that seemed as big as golf balls at that moment. She had a beautiful face, a long oval, tanned to a deep brown. Her eyelashes were long. At that moment if seemed impossible he'd ever mistaken her for a man.

"Are you going to take over?" she asked, moving away from him again.

"Yes. But Hawk left orders for you to help me. There are a lot of holes in this one. You should have some of the answers."

"So I get to work with the famous Nick Carter, the great Killmaster," she said, her voice flat, perhaps on the edge of sarcasm.

Carter decided to ignore the hostility. He knew she was hurting inside. "I'm just a man with a job to do. I'd like your help."

She managed a wan smile. "I'm sorry. You're right. But I might not be myself for a while."

"That's okay. Tell me what you know. What about the Soo brothers?"

"Clowns who made it big. Two crazy Chinese with an idea for an elixir and they parlayed it into billions. They couldn't read or write, but they sure knew how to make money. Have you ever seen Ginseng Essense Balm Park?"

"No."

"A tourist attraction. Filled with figures from Chinese mythology and superstition, and I suspect, some of their fantasies. The place is filled with characters undergoing various forms of torture, bodies ripped apart, children in bondage—that kind of thing. It's fascinating in a horrible sort of way," she said, pulling on her cigarette, "but the tourists eat it up."

The brandy had taken effect. She slid down in the bed and snuggled against him, under one arm. She talked up at him, her voice dulled at times, animated at others. He could feel the heat of her. Involuntarily he thought of her as he'd seen her before her bath. She'd been beautiful even when she'd been filthy. He forced his mind back to the job at hand.

"So who took them?" he asked.

"We don't have conclusive proof, but I'm fairly sure it was Fat Chen."

Carter's mind slipped back to his friends in Hong Kong, the Chen clan and his old friend Two Toe Chen, now long dead. The name Chen was like Smith. Fat Chen, wherever he came from, was probably no relation. "Tell me about him," he said.

"Arthur Cecil Chen. Adopted by missionaries and christened with names they gave him. They were killed by hill bandits in northern Thailand. Fat Chen came here as a teen-ager, worked the docks as a peddler, got into the drug trade, and built it into a billion-dollar business."

"An entrepreneur?"

"No. More of a robber baron. Ruthless. He controls most of the vice in Singapore, and rules by fear and torture. Hundreds of thugs work for him."

"Why the Soo kidnapping?" he asked, his right arm going to sleep under her. He shiftted her weight to his shoulder.

"Another grab for power. They were competitors in the drug trade," she said, moving next to him as she talked, her skin hot and soft. "Barney and I learned that the brothers had turned all their assets into cash, enough money to eliminate the deficit of most developing countries."

"And Chen planned to siphon it off."

"He probably already has," she said, shifting her weight against his shoulder, her head resting against his chest, her clean fragrance drifting up to his nostrils.

"Do you think the Soo brothers are dead?"

"Fairly sure. Barney had contacts in the financial community. The Soo money has probably been transferred to a series of dummy companies. Experts Barney knew figured that hundreds of businessmen would present bank drafts in the name of the brothers and the money would find its way into a labyrinth of paper companies. It's probably all been funneled back to Fat Chen by now."

"Are you sure of this?"

"No. But it's the best scenario. It's not the first like this we've seen. Barney knew of three other cases like this. He traced them back to Chen, but he couldn't make any of them stick. The Soo brothers were the big prize. The others were probably exercises to sharpen up Chen's people and set the plan."

"Where do I find Chen?"

"You don't. He doesn't operate in the open. There are lots of rumors about him."

"Like what?" he asked.

"Promise not to laugh. I'm dead serious. Okay?"

"Go ahead."

"Some say he's a monster controlling his empire through state-of-the-art technology. Everything he does is by video cameras and monitors. If he wants one group disciplined, he calls on another to do his dirty work. He has a tape file on everyone in his organization."

"Blackmail."

"Probably. I've heard he has video cameras in the offices of all his executives. If he has so many cameras out in the open, how many do you suppose he's got hidden?"

"What did you mean by executives?"

"He's got a huge legitimate conglomerate. He owns half of Singapore."

"Like what?"

She thought about it for a moment. "Take Chinatown alone. He owns fifteen to twenty of the most modern buildings: Hong Guan, Far East Financing, Asia Insurance Building, Chaing Hong Building. The list goes on and on. Half the junks plying the China Sea are his, most of the sampans in the harbor, a quarter of the freighters doing business out of the Lion City."

"Impressive. Where are his headquarters?"

"I've had a dozen answers on that one. Barney had it narrowed down."

"How?"

"He figured if Chen wanted total privacy to operate, he'd use a remote estate. He owns three. One on Telok Blangah Road near the Ginseng Essense Park, one on Pioneer Road near the Jurong Bird Park, and one on Lady Hill Road not a quarter mile from here."

"Did Barney have any hunches?"

"Barney was a pragmatist. I had the hunches, Carter. At first I thought it was the Lady Hill Road house because of the incredible security. But I checked the other two houses and found they had the same tight security."

"Example."

"Double fences with laser beams between. The fences are electrified and the lasers deadly."

"They can be circumvented," Carter thought to himself, but voiced the thought.

"There's more. He has robots like small tanks that patrol inside the fence. The lasers don't seem to restrict the movement of the robots."

"He probably has the lasers programmed to shut off momentarily as the robots pass."

"And he has robots inside the fence patrolling the grounds."

"On all three estates?"

"Yes."

"No matter. We'll find a weakness. What about the prime minister, Peter Hue Yen?" Carter asked.

"You're well informed. Yes," she said as if thinking ahead, "Hue Yen. He's been the salvation of Singapore."

"I know the place is a model of economic efficiency," Carter said, "but the people are like clones. You can go too far. The place is too rigidly controlled. Big Brother tells you how to live your life."

"I can only go by my experience, Carter. This place was a cesspool when the Japanese were driven out. Now it's a model for the world. So what if the people are regimented? They have the best standard of living in Southeast Asia."

"I didn't come here to argue politics. What are his politics, by the way?"

"Hue Yen is straight line. He controls his party and has one objective: to make Singapore the best."

"His assistant, Robert Quang," Carter persisted. "We think he's got Communist leanings."

"It goes much deeper than that," Samantha said, her voice stronger. She was more in control of herself now. "Robert Quang's influence stretches throughout the Malay Peninsula. He was the one who took over the Soo brothers' share of the drug trade before Chen got to them. It was a means of weakening the opposition and filling his war chest. He's the 'behind the scenes' leader of the People's Enlightenment Party, PEP. The party has climbed in popularity after long years of hard-fisted rule by the prime minister and his Independent Party.

"But that's all a closely guarded secret," she went on. "Quang has been Hue Yen's assistant for the last three years and now he's the logical man to succeed him. You're right about his real beliefs. We figured he's a deep plant of the KGB. Barney and I got too close, so he set us up. Or Chen did the dirty work for him."

"That expands on what Hawk told me. He said the prime minister and the U.S. secretary of state fear that someone was controlling the Soo fortune and could begin a dump of Singapore dollars on world markets. That could cause a crash in Singapore's economy and an open door for PEP. They also suspect that PEP is masterminded by someone privileged to the secrets of the prime minister's inner cabinet. Hawk didn't know it was Quang."

"We couldn't report to Hawk soon enough. Everything went down too fast at the end."

"So Quang is our first target."

"He could be the worst problem out here. I don't trust Quang. I know he's been trained at the Lumumba Institute in the USSR."

Carter whistled. "That piece of information is enough to get you killed."

"No one knows I have that juicy bit. I'm not doing anything about it, not now, but it could be useful in the long run."

"You think he's tied in with Chen?"

"It's a strong probability. That's what we were trying to check out when we were drugged and set up," she said, squirming into a more comfortable position beside him. "If Chen's usual plan was directed at Quang, he could be controlling him."

"But we already know that Quang is KGB," Carter noted.

"So he goes both ways," Samantha said. "But who has his loyalty? I'd bet on Chen's blackmail over the KGB."

"Did you see your abductors?"

"I saw them and I know who they are. But that doesn't do us one damned bit of good."

"No, but we could set up some surveillance, have someone on them at all times," Carter said. "We've got to find out for sure if Quang is connected with Chen. And we've got to find out if his real masters are the Russians."

"So we need someone on Quang as well?"

"I don't want to bring anyone else in on it if we can help it. It's up to you and me. We'll get what we want by ourselves and then close them down."

"Is that a promise?"

"No promises," Carter said, and laughed. "Now. What about clothes? I'll go down to the hotel boutiques when they open soon and get an outfit for you. You can do some shopping on your own later."

"Then you want me as a woman?"

Carter smiled at the phrasing. He'd been thinking about that very thing. He'd already concluded he wanted her as a woman in more ways than one.

"I want you to dress as a woman. Buy a wardrobe and a piece of luggage. We'll make sure we've got what we need, then we'll move," he said. "This place is too obvious for us. When you're outfitted, we'll move to the Lady Hill Hotel. You're going to visit a beauty salon for a wig or two and I'm going to get myself a makeup kit," he went on. "We'll have new names and identities. While they're looking for you as they remember you, we'll be installed in the Lady Hill, in the best suite, a rich American couple who don't resemble either of us in any way."

"Beautiful. I'm not sure I like the man and wife part. Why not father and daughter? And you'd better make sure the suite has two bedrooms. I'm not one of your pushovers."

FIVE

The Lady Hill Hotel couldn't be compared to the Shangri-la, but it was a safe haven for the time being. Carter took a small suite at Samantha's insistence. While she still seemed a little in awe of him, her reaction was the opposite of most females. It wasn't that she was totally indifferent; she seemed to need his closeness and comfort, or maybe it was protection. Carter decided to ignore the issue, if indeed it was an issue. He thought it might be refreshing to complete an operation without the complications of a sexual relationship with one of the principals.

"What are you going to do about your hair?" he asked as she knocked and entered his room.

"I noticed a beauty parlor here in in the street-level shopping mall. If they don't have wigs, they'll be able to find one."

"Try for a totally different coloring. Your face is tanned. It's a classic long oval. Find something that tones down your skin color and makes your face look rounder," he suggested.

"Most women have a nodding acquaintance with hairdos and makeup," she said dryly. "Don't worry, Carter, you won't know me."

"Just trying to help. You won't know me, either," he said. "I'm going on a shopping trip for a makeup kit and clothes for an older man. I'm going to be your father—gray hair, a short beard, stoop-shouldered."

"Where will we meet?"

"A good point. I like this place, but we can't stay. While I'm out I'll find another hotel. Any other suggestions?"

"Why not stay here? Change your appearance outside and register again under another name."

Carter grinned. Her stock just went up ten points. If for any reason the oher side had a line on them and they disappeared, the enemy would be combing the other hotels for them, not the same one. "I'll register as Goeffrey Smith-Wells, retired colonel of the Welsh Guards. You'd better forget about the beauty shop downstairs. We'll both have to be sure we have no one tailing us when we change our appearance."

"Why not Americans as we decided?"

"Take them further from the scent."

"Good idea. I'll be Caroline, your veddy uppah-crust daughter. Very spoiled snob type. Makes it all the more plausible when you ask for separate bedrooms."

"All right," Carter said. "Sounds good to me. Let's get going. I'll be back in two hours and signed in. You'd better arrive with a taxiload of boxes from local shops. How are you fixed for money?"

"Not one Singapore dollar."

He handed her a wad of bills and picked up the attaché case Schmidt had give him. He'd leave the rest of his clothes here and sign out when the action was over. He smiled at the thought. He was leaving bits and pieces of his wardrobe all over town. "That's it, then," he concluded. "You leave first. I'll follow in a few minutes.

Chen sat at his massive console, his equally massive buttocks spilling out of his chair. His voice, usually so loud it drowned out all other sound, had risen to the threshold of pain. "*You're telling me they are out of jail? Where are they?*" he roared, the wattles at the sides of his face shaking, his color three shades of crimson darker than usual.

"They were broken out by a professional, Excellency."

"Why do you say 'professional'?" he asked, the decibel level dropping a few points.

"He introduced a form of gas into the ventilation system, then went in dressed like an antiterrorist expert."

"And he got them both out?" Chen roared.

"No, Excellency," the voice of his underling came back, then hesitated. On the screen he looked afraid and confused. "Well, he got them out, but one was shot."

"What? Who shot?"

"Two police appeared on the scene. They shot one of the agents while the invader was moving the body to his car."

"Which one? Is he dead or alive?"

"The big one. He's dead."

"Did our people get a good look at the new one? What about the license of his car?"

"They saw him briefly. He was tall. That's all they can say. He was tall and strong."

Chen thought about the caliber of an enemy who could

put a whole building under his control and escape a maximum-security area with two prisoners. "How many police were killed?" he asked.

"None. He could have killed many, but he apparently didn't shoot to kill."

"Interesting," Chen said, his voice almost at a normal level, a whisper for him, as if he were talking to himself. "One man, tall and strong, takes two prisoners from the cellars of the Justice Building. He doesn't kill any police. What happened to the dead one?" he suddenly asked in his normal booming tones.

"Strange. The body is not in the local morgue. It was picked up by a foreign group."

"What foreign group? Do I have to drag it out of you one piece at a time?"

"It happened fast, Excellency. The body never got to the morgue. It was intercepted on the way and transferred to another van. We don't have a description. We were relying on our informant at the morgue."

"So one of them escaped and is with this tall strong man," Chen bellowed. "The small one escaped. That one was too nosy. I'm sure he knows more than he should. And now he's spilling his guts to a stranger—a very capable stranger," he fumed. "You know what that means, you fool?"

"No, Excellency."

"It means that instead of closing a gap in our armor, we have a new player in the game," he said, his voice like a whip. "Now, you listen to me. I want all our people at the hotels to keep an eye open. Every taxi driver and every pedicab driver must be on the alert. We know what the small one looks like. He's thin. His hair is short and a kind of dark red in color. His eyes are brown. Do we have pictures of him?"

"Not very good ones of him. All taken at a distance. What about your video tapes, Excellency? Did you have him on camera?"

"None of you have been bright enough to get him on camera for me," Chen roared. "Now, get busy and find them for me! Alert Quang. If we find them, he'll have to deal with them personally. I want to know what they know and what they've passed on."

"Yes, Excellency."

"Well, get busy! I want them by the end of the day!"

She called from the lobby and was knocking on his door within minutes. When he opened it for her, he was impressed. If he hadn't been expecting her, he'd have taken her for someone else.

In turn she looked at him, her mouth a round O, her eyebrows arched, before she came in timidly. "Carter?" she asked.

He laughed and waved her in. When they were in the privacy of the suite, they both stood, above five feet apart, and laughed in wonder. She was a blonde with a tawny complexion. She had used contact lenses to change her eyes to green. Her choice of clothes was perfect for the snooty daughter of a very old-fashioned, retired British military man.

Carter stood, his shoulders stooped, his skin a dark parchment, wrinkled by the tropic sun. He had not changed the length of his hair but had changed the color to a dull charcoal gray. His eyes were hidden behind tinted glasses with thick tortoiseshell frames. He had a small chin beard and a ragged mustache.

He waved her to a chair. "You've done well." As he spoke, a sharp rap on the door startled them.

"My clothes," she said.

Carter opened the door to a hall porter pushing a luggage cart laden with colorful boxes.

"I say, Caroline, must you buy out the shops everywhere we go?" Carter said for the benefit of the porter, his accent pure Oxbridge.

"Oh, Daddy. What do expect me to do in these dreadfully dull places?" Samantha said, playing her role of the spoiled daughter to the full.

Carter hesitated while the man waited, then reluctantly tipped him with one Singapore dollar, an amount that curled the man's lip and would brand the old British gentleman as a parsimonious old dinosaur.

When they were alone, Carter poured a couple of brandies from a decanter. As he handed one to Samantha he wasted no time on preliminaries. "I said we'd have to play this out alone. But I think we've got too many bases to cover alone," he said. "You said you had an in with the local police. How good is it? Can we trust your contact?"

"The best. Chief of Police Windsor. His close friends call him 'Chalkie.' I'm close but not that close."

"Does he know you're a woman?"

"He's about the only one who does."

"Tell me about him."

"Hue Yen met him long before he became prime minister. Chief Windsor was a military man but always in police work or intelligence. He took an early pension and was an acting superintendent of New Scotland Yard when Hue Yen persuaded him to move to Singapore."

"Hue Yen's a very shrewd character. Is Windsor that good?"

"He's about the best I've run across. And he prefers to be called '*Chief* Windsor,' by the way."

"Were there problems in the force? Jealousy from local men who thought they should have the job?"

"You don't know Hue Yen. His people know better than to complain," she said. "There probably was some underlying jealousy at first, but not when they got to know Chief Windsor."

"What about ego? Is Chief Windsor going to be a problem?"

"I don't think so. His wanting to be called Chief Windsor is just a quirk of his. How do you want to handle it?" she asked.

"We don't want to go to police headquarters and be spotted with him. Can you get him here?"

"I think so."

"Good. One more thing. What do you know about other police action here? Any complications?"

"No. Chief Windsor has total control. Hue Yen has never allowed any duplication of departments. He hates interdepartmental jealousies, and fires anyone who shows signs of empire building or moving in on another department."

"So Chief Windsor has a clear field."

"That's about it," Samantha said. "I'd be bothered with the autonomy with anyone else, but Chief Windsor handles it well. You'll see."

"Let's do it. Try to get him up here."

George Windsor was more low-key than Carter expected. Instead of the ex-military type in a military-cut suit or in a police uniform, Chief Windsor showed up at their door in a dark blue business suit, a striped tie that complemented his two-tone shirt, and expensive Italian loafers. He was smaller than Carter expected, just coming to Carter's chin. His hair was light brown, combed straight back. His brown eyes looked at the two of them through fashionable lightweight glasses. The eyebrows of his tanned, round face arched in surprise at their appearance.

"I told you I'd look different," Samantha said with a smile as she waved him to a chair.

"Let's get something straight from the start," Chief Windsor said as he sat and took the offered brandy. "I've worked with Sam before without digging too deeply into her background. I'm not going to do the same this time."

Carter and Samantha looked at each other. Neither spoke. Chief Windsor tried to outwait them but with no success. "I won't do it. You've already caused a furor in Kuala Lumpur. I don't like to hear about police being wounded doing their duty, even if they were not mine. I don't like working with the ones who shot them."

"It couldn't be helped, Chief Windsor," Carter explained. "I could have killed a half-dozen officers at the Justice Building and the job would have been a lot easier. I stuck my neck out to avoid hitting the police. If I'd been there to kill, Barney Feldman wouldn't have bought it."

Chief Windsor digested the answer and shifted his gaze to Samantha. "What the hell are you up to this time?"

"The same thing," Samantha said. "Robert Quang and whoever's behind him. Did you already know Barney was killed?"

She managed to say it and keep her composure, but Carter knew that it hurt. He was beginning to admire this woman more as time went on.

"My people were sent from here to get him. Did you know he was transferred to a private ambulance from our meat wagon before we got him to the morgue? Now, that takes some kind of clout. Just what the hell's going on, Samantha?"

"You know I can't open up all the way, Chief. This is a man who works as I do," she said, indicating Carter. "He's about twenty-five years younger than he looks. If we're going after Quang and Chen, we've got to be very careful."

"And who do you work for, Mr. Carter?"

"A man in Washington."

"What man?"

"A man close to the president."

"Do I take it you're not from one of the usual agencies?"

"That much I can tell you."

"Look here. I was superintendent of Special Branch before I came down here, worked with your CIA chaps all the time. I never heard of any clandestine agency then and I don't believe it now."

The silence in the room went on for what seemed like a full two minutes. "What the hell do you want with me?" Chief Windsor finally asked.

"I came here to take Samantha and Feldman out," Carter said. "But it goes deeper than that. If the other side set them up, they'll do everything in their power to do something like it again. I can't just leave it at that. You want the whole piece?"

"I don't have anything pressing at the moment," Chief Windsor said, holding out his empty snifter.

"You probably know this better than I," Carter started. "We think Quang is a pawn for the Soviets. Hue Yen isn't getting any younger. If Quang takes over, he opens the back door for Communism to infiltrate within weeks. Sin-

gapore goes, then the whole peninsula, Sumatra, Bali—
the whole area."

"That's my problem, Mr. Carter. What in bloody hell do
you think you can do?"

"Don't you ever feel your hands are tied, Chief Windsor? Have you ever arrested a major criminal and had him
get off with a suspension or less?" Carter knew he was on
firm ground. No police chief in the world had not experienced a ton of similar frustrations.

"You know damned well I have," Chief Windsor said in
his clipped accent. "What's the point?"

"Samantha and I can't cover all the bases. We want to
know who Quang sees night and day. We want to know
who he calls and who calls him," Carter recited. "He's the
assistant prime minister. It'll all have to be done with your
most trusted men."

Chief Windsor sat, twisting the brandy snifter in his
hand, taking his time. "It would be a problem if something
happened to Hue Yen and Quang took over. I'm no fool,
Carter. I know what he is. But he's damn close to the top.
I've got to move carefully."

"I know. But we've got to make sure of our facts. Suspi-
cions won't hack it. If we can be sure that Quang and Chen
are a threat to the area, I'll deal with them. You'll be
clean."

"Except to explain the mess you leave behind."

"You can't have it both ways."

Samantha was letting them have it out. Now she joined
in. "I was telling Nick about Chen's background. Have you
come up with anything new lately?" she asked.

"Nothing you don't know."

"What about his electronics expertise?" Carter asked.
"How does he get his supplies? Surely we can put a watch

on his estates and pin down his operating headquarters."

"I've not seen Chen in years, Carter. My people give me rumors about him growing immensely fat and being unable to move in a normal society. He's been know as Fat Chen for years, but I understand he's twice the size now that he used to be."

"*If* your information's correct," Carter reminded him. "Samantha thinks he's set himself up in a high-tech wonderland where he keeps an eyes on his empire by video."

"She's probably right," Chief Windsor said.

"State-of-the-art surveillance is so sophisticated it's scary," Carter reminded them. "He could have miniature cameras hidden where they'd never be suspected. He could even have some concealed on his people. Makes you wonder," Carter went on. "How clean is your office, Chief Windsor? And your home? When was the last time you had an electronic sweep of them?"

Chief Windsor blanched at the suggestion and was thoughtful for a minute or two. Carter and Samantha didn't disturb his thoughts.

"All right. My people will concentrate on Quang and Chen. What will you be doing?" he finally asked.

"Leave the surveillance of Chen's mansions to us," Carter said. "Keep an eye on his enterprises. Watch for Soviet contacts."

Chief Windsor rose to leave. "Anything else?" he asked.

"We seem to have conflicting information on who controls the drug rackets," Carter said. "We heard that the Soo brothers were in competition with Chen, and that would be motivation enough for Chen to get rid of them. We also heard that Quang eased the Soo brothers out of drug traf-

ficking before they were abducted. That would make him a
competitor with Chen and not an ally."

"Unless Chen used Quang to take down the Soo
brothers and Quang is merely running part of the drug trade
for Chen," Chief Windsor offered.

"The whole thing's too damn complicated," Carter said.
"It just proves we can't operate without intelligence."

"Just what did you come here for, Carter?" Chief Windsor asked. "You said it was to spring your people. Now
you've got your nose in the Soo business."

"We lost two CIA men just after the kidnapping. My
people want to know who has the Soo brothers and why."

Chief Windsor had another of his pauses. Carter was
beginning to get used to them.

"Samantha and I might have to change our appearance
more than once," Carter said, finally breaking the silence.
"We may have to move around. So we'll get in touch with
you."

Chief Windsor seemed to come out of deep thought,
resigned and willing to cooperate. He pulled a business
card from an inner pocket and added a special number.
"I'm here most of the time. If not, a machine will answer
and I check it every hour."

"If you don't hear from us in twelve hours, come looking," Carter added.

But the policeman had the last word. "I'm going along
with this because we've got very grave problems, Carter. I
know I can't handle it by conventional means. But if you
cross me in any way, *any way at all*, I'll have your hide,"
he said.

His eyes left no doubt about his intent. He was a good
man to have on your side, Carter decided, but not one to
have against you.

"How did Hue Yen ever settle on him as his chief of police?" Carter asked when Chief Windsor had left. "Didn't he have his whole party on his back to put some local man in that position?"

"You obviously don't understand the Hue Yen power structure," she said. "He chooses whom he wants and he tells his cabinet they can go along or get out. With his unique background, Chief Windsor is better at what he does than any local could be. That's not just my bias. They all respect him—and fear him, Carter. He's a good man—a good one to have on your side."

"He's close to Hue Yen?"

"I understand he has the prime minister's ear whenever he needs it."

"Good. I have a feeling we'll need old Chalkie's help before this is over."

The front entrance to the Lady Hill Hotel was jammed with vehicles as Chief Windsor strode out to his waiting car. He swung in swiftly and his driver pulled out of the snarl of traffic into the Lady Hill flow as only an expert driver was capable.

A black Mercedes pulled out of its spot near the entrance and followed, keeping a hundred yards between the two vehicles.

"What did you find out inside?" the passenger, a big man, asked in Russian.

"He visited the seventh floor. The two we want are on the fifth floor."

"I smell something here, Sergei," the passenger said. "It doesn't add up. We know the American woman agent has been friendly with Chief Windsor in the past. The Lady Hill Hotel has never figured in any action before. In the same day, we watch the woman move in with another American and Chief Windsor visit an entirely different room. What does that tell you?"

The smaller man was concentrating on his driving. As Chief Windsor's car approached police headquarters he kept on going and visibly relaxed. "What are you getting at, Yuri Alexandrovich? You think the same couple has two rooms?"

"What else could the answer be? Has the Lady Hill suddenly become a nest of vipers? No. I think not," he said smugly. "Our American friends are trying to be deceptive."

"And our next move?"

"Turn back to Lady Hill, Sergei Anatole, my friend. Find out who has registered on the seventh floor in the last few hours. If you find only one or two couples, put a team of our people on them. I want to know what they do every hour around the clock."

SIX

The car they rented was a small, unremarkable Toyota, a carbon copy of thousands on the streets of the Lion City. It was parked outside the Chen mansion on Telok Blangah Road near the Ginseng Essence Balm Park. They had decided not to observe one of Chen's properties a few blocks from their hotel first. To stay at the hotel and park just up the street for hours would seem unusual, even to the dullest mind.

"We haven't seen any action for hours," Samantha complained. She sat behind the wheel, her crisp new appearance slightly wilted, the wig a hot and bothersome addition in a car with no air conditioning.

"We can't expect any for hours," Carter said. He wasn't any more comfortable than his companion. The facial makeup, the wrinkled skin, was beginning to soften from his perspiration. The beard and mustache were sodden as the car heated up more and more under an unrelenting sun.

The interior smelled of stale cigarettes and body heat.

"We should have chosen a different disguise for this kind of work," Samantha offered. She opened the door and stepped out to stretch her legs.

In an action that caught them both off guard, a black Mercedes swept up beside them, its tires sliding on the soft asphalt. A man jumped out and caught Samantha with one arm around her throat. He had a deadly-looking automatic at her temple in seconds.

A second man moved out of the car. He seemed to be in no hurry. He walked to Carter's side of the car, keeping well clear of his partner, and pointed the barrel of a Makarov at Carter's head. "You will get out of the car slowly," he said.

With Samantha under their control, Carter didn't reach for a weapon. "See here," he said in the British accent he had adopted. "Now, see here. We're British. I'll have the consulate after you—"

"Stop the act, Mr. Carter," the big man growled. "Get in the back of our car with your 'daughter.' We have a few things to discuss."

Carter estimated the ride took a little more than twenty minutes. He'd been blindfolded and his hands were tied behind his back. He tried to remember all the stops and turns, but their frequency soon made that impossible. Some random smells he remembered: the rotting vegetables of a market; the fish and oil smell of the harbor; the faint whiff of an opium pipe when they had stopped to make a turn.

It had all added up to nothing useful. He decided to ride it out, as he'd done countless times before, find out who his enemies were, and wait for a break. But he had the added responsibility of the woman. Samantha had not made a sound during the ride. He was sure she was not unconscious and he doubted she'd been gagged.

They seemed to be moving slowly between buildings when the car stopped. He was pulled out of the car and pushed, stumbling, across the threshold of a building. He was shoved into a wooden chair and the blindfold was yanked off.

"Moscow will be delighted to know that we have the notorious Nick Carter," the big man said. He had discarded his coat and stood in front of Carter in a sweat-stained shirt, his baggy pants held up by wide black suspenders.

Samantha was in a chair beside Carter, her eyes downcast. She was shaking from fear. It was always worse for a woman. She never knew if her captors were crude enough to violate her.

As if to prove his point, three men entered and started to grin at the sight of the woman. One of them grabbed at her hair and laughed wildly as it came off in his hand.

"What do you want?" Carter asked, trying to get their attention from the woman.

The big man who had held the gun on Carter seemed to be in charge. He shouted at the others to stand back. "All in good time, comrades," he said. "First we will see what we have here. Strip them both and tie them to the chairs."

Rough hands grabbed at him. He couldn't see what was happening to Samantha, but he could hear her cries of protest. As they pulled off his coat and were working on the belt of his trousers, he turned to see them rip her dress down the front. Her small breasts heaved with her shouted curses as they shredded the rest of her clothes.

"So the great Killmaster has the 9mm Luger and the stiletto as we were told," the big man drawled. "How does it feel to be at the end of your journey at last, Carter?"

"Who the hell are you?" Carter asked, stalling for time, looking for a chance to make a break, any kind of a break.

"Colonel Yuri Alexandrovich Petrov at your service, Mr. Carter," the big man answered in Russian. "Komitet Gosudarstvennoy Bezopasnosti, First Chief Directorate, Executive Action Department."

"*Mokrie dela*" Carter said in the same language.

"*Mokrie dela*," Petrov said, his face broadening in a smile. "'Wet affairs.' You know what wet affairs are, Carter. You have killed enough of my comrades to know the expression well," he shouted at his captive, smashing a massive fist to the side of Carter's face. "The dreaded Killmaster. N3. Licensed to Kill.

"Well, I'm licensed to kill, too, Mr. Carter!" he shouted, then went on in a more normal tone. "I've been trained at the best places. Serbsky, Mr. Carter. You have heard of the Serbsky Institute?"

"Very crude, Petrov. Any fool can learn to fry a brain with drugs."

His ploy was working. Petrov hit him again with his bare fist and screamed at the men to leave. "I'm going to give you a few minutes to contemplate your death, Mr. Killmaster. But you will die," he said, giving each word emphasis. "Have no doubt of that. None. You will die, but not before you tell us all about the inner workings of AXE."

"A Soviet dog hiding behind a fat man and a politician," Carter taunted him as he was about to leave.

"What do you know, fool?" Petrov snarled as he walked back to face Carter. "The fat man has a very short time to live. The politician is another thing. He's one of us. Trained at Lumumba. He will be our figurehead in all of Malaysia."

"You sound confident, Petrov. Why tell me this? It confirms what I needed to know."

"Because you're a dead man, Carter. A dead man," he repeated as he closed the door after him.

Carter looked at Samantha for the first time. Her chin was on her chest. She was crying silently, not understanding a word they had said, bound up in the fear of death. Carter's heart went out to her. She, too, was naked. Her skin was rubbed raw where they had ripped her clothes from her. Bruises had started to show where they had grabbed at her breasts and inner thighs.

She was bald. Apparently she'd opted to remove all her hair to accommodate the wigs. It was a good sign. If she were that dedicated to her job, what had to be done now might not be impossible.

"Are you all right?" he asked in a whisper.

"What the hell kind of question is that?" she snapped at him. Maybe he'd been wrong. She seemed petrified by her circumstance. But they had to get out of there.

He took a deep breath and tried again. "Are you a good swimmer?" he asked.

"What are you getting at, Carter?"

"Well, are you?"

"I was in the Olympic trials at sixteen."

"Still have the lung power?"

"Yes. I'm into aerobics."

"Good," he said, slipping the ropes that held his wrists. He'd been working on loosening them since he'd been tied up.

"How did you do that?"

"Never mind," he grunted, untying his legs from the chair and moving to untie hers. She started to get up but he pushed her back.

"What's going on, Carter? Let's get out of here."

"We wouldn't get ten feet." He lifted one leg to reveal the tiny bomb. He peeled away the tape and held Pierre in his hand.

"What the hell's that?" she asked.

"Sit in your chair as if you were still tied," he said, putting his hands behind him as he spoke. "We want to look natural when they come back."

"What is that thing, Carter?"

"A gas bomb. One whiff is lethal. That's why I asked about your lung power."

"What are you going to do?"

"I know them. Petrov will be busy right now boasting to his superiors, but they'll be back soon. He'll want me to spill my guts and he'll give you to his men as part of my softening-up process."

She looked better, actually smiled as she contemplated a chance for freedom.

"Don't look so happy," he said. "They might be back any second. Keep your head down as you had it before. They won't see the missing rope."

"But how will I know when you're are going to do it?" she asked, moving her chin back to almost touch her chest.

"I'll let Petrov rant and rave for a minute or two—let the rest of them ogle you. If their blood is up, they won't suspect anything and they'll get a lungful of the gas right away."

"But what will I do?"

"When I yell 'Now!' I'll give you two seconds to take a deep breath and I'll drop the bomb in front of them," he told her. "Don't wait for them to go down. Get to the door and out as fast as you can. Don't wait for me."

"Don't wait? What will you be doing?" she asked, obviously concerned for him.

"Don't worry about me. I want to be sure they are all dead. We don't want any pursuers. When you get clear, look for my weapons and some clothes for us."

They heard feet pounding down the hall and raucous laughter. Carter said no more. Samantha hadn't survived for as long as she had without a keen intelligence. She would do all right.

From the moment they all trooped in, Carter could see the scenario wasn't going to go as he planned. One of the men grabbed at Samantha and she slipped off her chair. They all stared, dumbfounded, as they saw she was untied.

"Now!" Carter yelled. He took a deep breath, turned the two halves of Pierre, and let the small bomb drop on the floor in front of him.

Samantha sat for a moment, then bolted for the door. One of the men made a halfhearted grab for her, but his lungs were already full of the gas and he slipped to his knees.

Petrov's face took on a look of surprise as he dropped the tray of syringes he'd been carrying and fell, his face bouncing off the wooden floor.

Carter sat, easily holding his breath while they fell, one by one.

One man remained. He was a bull of a man, and looked like a Georgian farmhand or a circus strongman. Carter came up out of the chair and sank his fist in the man's stomach. It was like hitting a stone wall.

One rocklike arm swung at Carter's head. He tried to duck but it caught him at the temple and lifted him off his feet. He managed to hold his breath as he hit the far wall and slid to the floor.

The human tank came at him. He lashed out with a booted foot at Carter's thigh. The strength of the kick swung Carter around as the shock of the contact and the pain ran up the nerves of his spine.

The Killmaster's hands reached out for something to use as a weapon. His right hand closed on a chair leg. While his head throbbed from hitting the wall, he mustered up all his strength and brought the seat around in an arc, the solid middle of the chair catching the young giant in the groin. He went down, gulping his last breath.

Carter knelt where he was for a moment, trying to orient himself, then he struggled to his feet. He didn't know how long it had been since he'd dropped Pierre. He was starting to feel weak as spots flashed in front of his eyes.

He searched the fallen men carefully. He found none of his possessions but took one of the weighty Makarovs as a precaution.

Carter stumbled out the door and down the hall. Samantha wasn't alone. One of the Russians, a man no bigger than she was, was struggling with her for a gun. As Carter came on the scene, the man broke loose, the gun in his hand. He pointed it at the woman, an evil grin on his face.

The gun in Carter's hand boomed out its challenge and the small man went down, half his head blown away. But Carter was fading fast. His head was spinning from the first blow of the young giant. The wall he'd hit had done the worst damage. His vision began to blur. The last thing he saw was a nude woman, her hand to her mouth. Conscious thought sank into blackness as he reached out for her.

Samantha stood swaying in the house that she'd thought would be her tomb. Nick Carter had saved them, but he'd just passed out. *O God! Don't let him leave me now*, she thought. Then her sense of survival took charge. Still naked, she picked up one of the guns and searched the rest of the house. She found nothing incriminating, but picked up Carter's weapons. She looked out the windows. They were closed in by other buildings. No one had heard the shot, or if anyone had, he was ignoring it.

Next she knelt beside Carter and felt his pulse. It was strong. Good. Blood ran from his temple and he had a massive bruise forming on one hip. He might have a concussion, but he'd probably come around.

What was her first move? She found a pair of coveralls that was several sizes too big, but she pulled them on and rolled up the legs. She found a coat that almost fit her, buckled on a pair of sandals, and covered her head with a canvas sun hat. She felt more human.

Again she examined Carter. He hadn't moved. She looked around and found his old-man clothes in the closet of an upstairs room. They would have to do. It seemed to take forever to dress him, including the Luger and the stiletto. He still had a wad of Singapore currency in his pocket. She transferred it to her coat pocket and tried to get him on his feet.

He moaned and hung on to her shoulders. She propped him up by the door while she looked out into the street. The people were all Chinese. Considering that three quarters of the city's population was ethnic Chinese, that didn't mean anything. But these people were different. They were dressed in more traditional garments.

Chinatown.

She recognized the top of a temple. It was the distinctive Wak Hai Cheng Bio Temple. They were at the back of the holy building. So they had to be somewhere near Canal Road or George Street.

What would be the best hotel for them? she wondered. Something not far away and not too big. The Furama. Somehow, some way, she'd take him to the Furama.

Samantha hoisted Carter and started to move. His brain responded in low gear and his feet moved with her, not taking all his weight, but at least she didn't have to drag him.

It seemed like an eternity but was probably only a few minutes before she found herself on George Street. A cab stopped at her frantic signal.

"Help me with this useless drunken husband," she screamed at the taxi driver in gutter Cantonese.

"I don't want blood on my seats, woman," the driver shouted over his shoulder, starting to take off.

"Fifty dollars, you son of a sampan whore," she yelled at him.

He backed up, snatched the fifty from her hand—about thirty-five American dollars—but didn't get out to help her with her burden.

With help, Carter slipped into the back, knocking his head against the roof. Samantha tried to guide him, cursing all the while.

"Take me to the Furama Hotel, you helpless excuse for a man," she continued to rail at the reluctant driver.

The hotel clerk was about to give her the same treatment when she threw a hundred-dollar bill at him and grabbed the key out of his hand.

"I'll need two nights in advance," he told her, his face devoid of expression. "Five hundred dollars."

"Your mother was a Shanghai whore," she snapped at

him in Cantonese. While trying to hold up Carter, she peeled off five bills.

No one in the lobby paid any attention or tried to help as she pulled her useless husband to the elevators. The elevator and the hall of the fourth floor were both empty as she opened the door to room 450 and dragged Carter inside.

When he was on the bed she sat in a chair and cried. She'd been through a hell of a lot for the CIA and for AXE, but never anything like this. How many Russians had he killed? At least six with the gas and one he'd shot defending her.

She stopped sobbing and wiped her eyes. He looked comfortable enough. She couldn't go for a doctor, so she filled an empty ice bucket with warm water and washed the blood from his face. It was all she could do for him for now.

The bathroom was old-fashioned but the tub was a monster. It had ancient plumbing, all chrome, with an oversize mixer on the wall above the tub. She wiped the bath clean and turned on both faucets. The mixer soon had a steady stream of hot water filling the tub, the temperature constant.

Samantha peeled off her clothing and climbed into the tub. The water closed over her like hot mercury, easing her muscles. The tension seeped out of her as she gave herself up to her thoughts. . . .

My God, that was close. If it weren't for Nick, I'd have been gang raped, probably dead. He is all they say he is and more. With any other man . . .

She never finished the thought as her mind went back to the last time. Three black youths and three white in the basement of a tenement in Brooklyn. Twelve hours of constant abuse and torture. It hadn't been enough that they had taken her, each of them, many times, it was the foul things they had forced her to do to them afterwards; at knifepoint, while onlookers watched. . . .

She had been in the hospital in Manhattan for a month. She'd gone home to Maine, to her family, but it hadn't helped. She returned to Manhattan, studied Oriental martial arts and earned a closetful of black belts, visited a shrink twice a week for two years without him helping much, then was persuaded by a friend to join the Central Intelligence Agency.

She had tried it with two men since, but it had not worked. Each time, at the last minute, the six faces would loom up in front of her and she would end up screaming and fighting off her would-be lover.

She still had urges. The psychiatrist had explained it to her. Her libido would be her worst enemy. She would want to have sex with a man, but her memories would always block her. She knew she'd prove him wrong someday.

Samantha stepped from the tub, dripping. She toweled herself dry and tiptoed into the bedroom. Carter was as she had left him. As she looked at the nasty gash across his temple, she felt a flow of tenderness toward him, and a warm feeling filled her loins.

She had to do something for him. She'd give him a sponge bath. Samantha filled the ice bucket with lukewarm water again, pulled off his clothes gently, and started to run the soft, lathered cloth over his body.

The feeling was strangely sensual. Both of them naked —she ministering to him.

The bruise on his hip looked nasty. She was extra careful with it. His body was tan and muscular, covered with scars, some recent, some puckered and old. The warmth between her legs grew to send a flush all the way to her face. Blood throbbed in her temples. She felt faint. She had never felt this way before in her life.

She'd had two men before the rape. One a youth in the back seat of a car when she was seventeen, one a married man, her first boss in the big city. The encounters had been disappointing. Both men had left her aroused and unsatisfied.

As Samantha ran the cloth over the tape marks that had held the small gas bomb near his genitals, she realized that while his mind was on hold, Carter's physical reflexes were still functioning. She started to finish the job, but her ministrations only added to what she'd already started.

Carter was not fully in control of his senses, but he knew who was touching him. He felt his natural instincts take over as the sensuous movements of her hands sent messages from his loins to his brain.

"It's all right," he kept telling himself. "This is not the enemy," his brain repeated over and over. What was happening to him wasn't dangerous.

Samantha watched him react to her touch and felt herself growing warmer and filled with desire.

"Samantha," he whispered, his eyes still closed.

"He's thinking about me. He's unconscious but he's thinking of me. Her knees began to give way and she slumped on the bed next to him, the wet cloth dropping to the floor.

The weight of her on the bed turned him slightly and one hand reached out for her.

This was madness, she thought. He wasn't conscious. She couldn't . . .

Despite the warm bath, she began to shiver. Something

drove her on. She *needed* this and he was the first man who had not frightened her . . . the first.

She moved closer. She shivered again. She felt herself pressed against the length of him, felt the hardness of him against her flank, the warmth of his flesh.

"Samantha," he said again, running a hand over her small breasts, bringing the tips of her nipples to a hardness she had never felt before.

A warmth suddenly poured through her and she felt as if her loins were about to explode. She reached for his hand and placed it on her belly, opening her legs for him.

The sensation of his hand moving on her was almost more than she could stand. It was the most sensual feeling she'd ever experienced. It encompassed her, flooding her senses, sending the blood to her head. She moaned, then almost cried out as a wave of passion overwhelmed her.

"Samantha," Carter mumbled, his hand working its way between her legs and caressing her until she felt she'd go mad. . . .

Just this once . . . let it happen . . .

As if her prayer were answered, one powerful arm swept her on top of him, her legs spread around him, absorbing him totally.

Samantha thought she was going to die with the joy of it. Slowly, so slowly it was almost more than she could bear, he began to move within her. He took the taut flesh of her rump in each hand and moved her in a slow, erotic dance of desire. It lifted her to a new level of ecstasy and she could no longer be patient. She moved faster, urged him on, forced his body to keep up with hers . . .

Carter was in a dreamland with a beautiful woman, a desirable woman, Samantha, on top of him. His brain wouldn't allow him full access to rational thought, but permitted his senses to run wild.

Was he all right? Deep inside his unconscious he knew he was safe. This was Samantha. This was paradise seen through a fog but felt with a clarity that drove him on.

It was so good, so much better than she had ever imagined. She moved above him, slapping her flesh against his flesh, not caring that he had stopped moving.

Then he began to moan. She realized that even in his condition she was going to bring him to a climax. The thought magnified her own feelings tenfold and the realization took her even higher. She moved like a wild woman until she reached a crest with him and cried out her joy. She didn't care if the whole hotel knew of her joy, the whole of Chinatown. The fires that had roared within her started to recede. She stopped moving and lay on top of him, her sweat-slick skin plastered to him.

He held her. Every minute or so his lips would move to sound her name: "Samantha."

She felt better than she had in her whole life. She felt normal . . . at last. Hadn't he mentioned her name throughout their lovemaking? He had helped her. He'd known she was there.

But she would have to tell him about it in the morning. They would do it again, but this time had been special. Never again would the fires of a private hell be burned away to reveal pure passion instead of the scars she'd worn.

SEVEN

The morning sun shone on them as they began to stir. It was hot. They lay naked on top of the sheets.

"I had the most incredible dream last night," Carter said as Samantha leaned over him.

"What was it?" she asked.

"I remember holding you close . . . in this bed. It was beautiful," he said, a huge grin on his face. "I was in a kind of dreamworld where an extraordinarily sensuous woman made love to me."

"Oh?" she said, smiling at him.

"Too bad it was just a dream," he sighed, rolling toward her on one elbow, looking her in the eye. "It seemed so real. Did we . . . ?"

She giggled, relieved that he had been conscious of their action. "Yes. We did." Then she suddenly became serious. "I needed you. I really needed you," she said, a tear flowing from one eye.

"Then I thank you for the beautiful experience," he said formally, a wicked smile on his face. "What do you think? Should we . . . ?"

In answer, she came into his arms, her mouth claiming his.

Chen was at his console in the early morning, scanning the monitors with a practiced eye. He had not left his chair all night but had taken two or three catnaps, the chair tilted back, the massive arms crossed over his chest.

The viewing was a routine matter. Not much action was taking place at that hour. Part of his brain was able to register every movement and sound from the countless sources available to him, while the other part took him back through time as it often did. His life had not been easy. To acquire the wealth he had, the road had been rough and he'd learned to be just as rough, to handle each situation with a cold deliberation as it presented itself.

His story had started early. When the only parents he'd known—an extremely sanctimonious Christian missionary couple who had dictated his every move—had died a violent death at the hands of hill bandits in Thailand, he was free to make his own way, but without one dollar to start him on the kind of path they would have wanted for him. More often than not, starting from absolute zero took a desperate soul down the path of least resistance. It was easier to steal from unsuspecting tourists than to find a job that would break his back for enough money to fill his stomach. He'd had three choices: take what he wanted, work for it, or beg for it. After years of exposure to preaching about God's way, words that had been unending and fallen on deaf ears, the choice had been no contest.

But the way had not been easy. In Singapore, with Hue

Yen in power, and it seemed as if he had been in power forever, the rule was work hard, stay clean and sober, and honor the rights of others. Someone was always at your side telling you the "right thing to do," the industrious way to contribute to the society, what to wear and what to say. And there were the "what nots." What not to say or do. It was not difficult for a bright young Chinese teen-ager to see that life would be easier and richer for him if he were as industrious as they preached—but that energy channeled in the direction of illicit rather than the puritan way of Hue Yen's doctrine. Perhaps it was a continuation of the preaching, the constant regimentation, that had turned him on his path. He'd had enough preaching. Freedom and wealth were his objectives, and he went after them with a vengeance.

He wasn't alone. Thousands of displaced young people fought for their daily livelihood in the streets and alleys of Singapore, even in Hue Yen's "perfect society." But the big youth had been just a little craftier than the rest, just a little quicker than the others, and much more ruthless. His movement to the top had been slow. Sometimes the leaps from plateau to plateau seemed huge, but as he grew prosperous, then rich, each plateau was not enough. A disease gnawed at him, pushed him on to new heights, showed him that a million was a pittance, a billion not an unreasonable objective, the control of Malaysian wealth not impossible.

He'd been only seventeen when he killed his first man. With the enemy out of the way, he was able to expand. It was a valuable lesson. Men of his kind were loners, backed by empty-headed lieutenants who were not leaders. Cut off the head and the prize was easy to take.

Soon it was no problem to justify the deaths of whole families to purge an enterprise of leadership. The end justified the means; that rationalization closed the door on conscience.

It had been a lonely climb through the years. He could trust no one. Machines were more reliable and had no conscience. Electronic technology advanced so rapidly, it was the only medium that could match his greed, his compulsion to have it all.

The more he used the miracle electronic chip to his advantage, the less he came into contact with human beings. His psyche called out for a substitute and found a release in food. The rawboned youth took on pounds and moved more slowly. He lost his hair after a bout with a rare fever, another reason to shun other people. The image changed from a tall, muscled youth to a huge, shiny-domed and evil gargoyle, a face that never smiled, eyes that looked more reptilian than human. Fat Chen was born after the first hundred million and dropped out of sight.

Men like Chief Windsor had tried to bring him to justice, had pursued him unsuccessfully from the first day he had taken the easy road, but Chen had never left evidence of his crimes, was never present, and rid himself of any possible connection to illegal acts by the simple process of ending a life . . . or as many as it took to achieve his ends.

The huge gleaming dome shone in the glow of a hundred monitors. He shook his huge frame in the monstrous chair and rid himself of the memories that haunted him. This was his life, carefully chosen and gained only after years of fighting, one difficult, hate-filled step at a time.

He keyed in the image of a youthful Japanese at work in a laboratory. "Have you completed the improvements on my robots?" he asked, his voice filling the room like the rumble of thunder directly overhead.

"They are not ready. The ones guarding you are state of the art. You should have no fears."

"You will never use the word 'fear' when talking to me! And you will address me as 'Excellency'!" the voice boomed out.

The small Japanese was silent. He had always been uncommunicative. Chen knew the reason. The fool thought he was indispensable, that he had only to delay improvements on his current project and hint about new marvels to stay alive. He was brilliant and he was also a fool. No one was indispensable. Another genius could be found and bound to Chen's service.

"I give you until tomorrow," he said. "The improvements will be in place tomorrow or you are a dead man."

Chen keyed in another monitor. Three Chinese men in their twenties sat around a table playing cards, their ashtrays filled with mashed but still smoldering butts.

"What of the American?" he demanded.

"The new man and the one he took from jail were taken by the Soviets—" one of the men started to explain.

"*What*?? How could you permit such a thing to happen?" he shouted in Cantonese, the sound of his voice almost ear-splitting.

"Permit me to explain, Excellency. The new one is a dangerous foe. He escaped after killing all the Russians. But they injured him in some way. He seemed to be dazed and the woman helped him to a taxi."

"The woman? What woman?"

"The small one he took from jail was a woman. She took him to a hotel."

"What hotel? Do I have to drag every word from your unworthy lips?"

"The Furama, Excellency. Even now they are in bed in their room."

The huge man pondered the news. So he was dealing with a new enemy, a dangerous one. He grinned, the flesh of his round face spreading as seldom-used muscles curled his features into a smile. One man and a weak woman. And as a bonus they had destroyed the organization the Soviets had painstakingly set up in his territory. The new man had been hurt in the process. The woman was a nonentity that could be crushed underfoot any time he wished, or could be given to one of his people as a reward.

"Take them."

"Yes, Excellency. Where would you have us take them?"

The mass of flesh that was a human being shook with glee as he developed the plot. "Take them to the House. Quang will inteview them. I will talk to him."

"Anything else, Excellency?" the man asked while the other two remained silent, frozen by their fear of the man who held them as slaves to his bidding.

"Yes. The Japanese is no longer of use to me. Make sure he has completed revisions to the robots and get rid of him."

Carter rolled over on his back and lit a cigarette. Samantha's deep breathing was the only sound in the room. He reached for the telephone and dialed Chief Windsor.

"Where the hell've you been?" the police asked without preliminaries.

"A long story. We were taken by a group of Russians, but we managed to get away."

"That's the kind of understatement my people are famous for," Chief Windsor said, not at all pleased. "I counted seven dead. I don't need this kind of trouble, Carter."

"What would you have had me do? They took us. They were about to rape Samantha and shoot me full of drugs. We'd have both ended up dead."

"But seven dead. How the bloody hell did you manage it?"

"Professional secret. I'll tell you about it one day. Right now I'm interested in your opinion," Carter said, bringing the conversation around to the direction he wanted it to go. "Were the Russians sent by Robert Quang? Were they acting on their own? Are there more of them?" he asked. "What do you think?"

"I think you've cleaned out their nest and someone's going to be bloody upset. I don't think they were sent by Quang. On the other hand, you may have played right into Chen's hands. One less factor for him to consider."

"So what do you think he'll do?"

"Hunt you down. Get you out of his hair. Where are you, by the way?"

Carter considered the wisdom of telling the man where he was on the hotel phone, but figured that if someone were listening in, it would have to be at the Furama switchboard. "I had a small concussion. Samantha managed to get me as far as the Furama Hotel."

"Are you all right now, old chap?"

"No more than a slight headache. Nothing a good breakfast won't cure."

"I'd advise you to find another hole to crawl into. They may be on to you there."

"Any word on Chen's exact location?" he asked.

"No. I'm sorry. My people haven't been able to pick up one clue."

"Okay. We'll establish another base and get in touch. Any suggestions?"

"I'm in the background as far as your activities are concerned, Carter. You're on your own," Chief Windsor said. "One last thing," he added. "We've long suspected Chen has a special place where he holds and interrogates enemies. A lot of our citizens disappear each year and we suspect they end up in his hands."

"Where is this place?" Carter asked.

"My people haven't been able to find it for me. But they've heard it referred to as 'the House.'"

"Sounds ominous. Let me know if you locate it."

"You may find it before I do if you don't watch your back, Carter," the police chief said, then paused for a long moment. "Take care of Samantha. She's quite a woman."

"That she is. We'll watch ourselves," Carter said as he hung up.

So he was no further ahead, he thought, as he mulled over his circumstances. Maybe he was. He'd had three enemies and now he had only two—as far as he knew.

They had to get out of there. But to where? He decided on the Lady Hill Hotel again. Why not? He was still registered in three suites, one at the Shangri-la and two at the Lady Hill. He swung from the bed and began to dress.

"What . . . what're you doing?" a sleepy voice from the bed asked.

"Get dressed. We're vulnerable here. We're going back to the Lady Hill."

She moved with speed once she grasped the urgency. They had only what they'd worn to the hotel, so were in a taxi and cruising along Havelock Road in minutes.

Something was wrong, Carter told himself. Chen had eyes everywhere, could even control the drivers of every hired vehicle in the city. He looked through the back window of the cab from time to time and spotted not one but two possible pursuers.

"Stop here," he ordered the driver, tossing a Singapore twenty on the front seat and dragging Samantha out the door.

With her hand still in his he moved quickly into the lobby of the Miramer Hotel and to a side door he knew well. In a second taxi, he scanned the road behind them, then repeated the move in the Glass Hotel.

"Do you still think the Lady Hill is the best move?" she asked as they transferred to a third cab. "All this evasion won't help at all if they've got us spotted at the Lady Hill."

"You could be right." They had been speaking in English. "Do you speak French or German?" he asked.

"Both. My German's better than my French. "Why?"

"Because Chen could have every taxi driver in the city in his pocket," he answered in German. "From now on we're German tourists."

"Drop us at the Apollo Hotel," he told the driver in English, confirming that the man understood the language.

They took a pedicab back to the Miramer Hotel, walked through the lobby to the employees' exit at the loading dock, and walked across the street to the River View Hotel.

"How are we financially?" she asked.

"All right for now. I've got to get in touch with Howard soon. I need something delivered to the embassy. We'll get new financing then."

Registering as German citizens, Carter made quite a show about the airline's having lost their luggage and let everyone in the lobby know his overall opinion of the inefficiency of everyone in the city. It was a display of Teutonic superiority that brought him instant dislike and identified them solidly as demanding and complaining foreigners. It was as effective a disguise as the short lived Smith-Wells role, the very British father of the spoiled Caroline.

"What's the new plan?" Samantha asked as they ordered food and drinks from room service.

"I'm going to visit Robert Quang's house tonight. He'd be very foolish to have evidence at home implicating himself, but I can't afford to pass up an opportunity."

"I'm going with you."

"Not this time."

"What am I supposed to do?"

"You could call Howard. Tell him to send along those grenades he showed me. He'll know which ones I mean. I've got an idea I'm playing with, and they may be useful. Tell him to send at least a few dozen and the phosphorous ones he showed me."

"Anything else?"

"You've met Pierre. I'll need two more, one lethal. We want the delivery tomorrow morning and we need a new bankroll. If I'm not back by noon tomorrow, go to the embassy and take delivery."

She came to him and looked up into his eyes, concern evident on her face. "Why wouldn't you be back by noon?" she asked, holding him by the arms.

"I don't intend to be more than three or four hours, but you never now. One clue leads to another. "Do you know where I can pick up a black outfit for a night reconnaissance?"

"Hung Tue's on Boon Tat Street. He's one of ours. Tell him you're with me."

EIGHT

The house of Robert Quang was in Ardmore Park, coincidentally almost backing up against the small golf course of the Shangri-la Hotel where Carter was still a registered guest. The information had come from Chief Windsor after Carter's visit to Hung Tue. The small Chinese, one of Samantha's recruits, had supplied Carter with everything he needed including a decrepit old Ford Cortina. The police chief had also come up with the address of Quang's offices in the Tuan Sing Tower on Market Street.

The house was set back on five acres and surrounded by a fence. Carter circled the whole property and used powerful glasses to make sure he had all the information he could get before he went in. He saw no guards, no dogs, and no robots. The absence of security could mean a supremely confident man or one who used highly sophisticated protection devices.

Carter donned the goggles Hung Tue had provided.

They could detect laser beams and showed that the house was crisscrossed on all sides by laser beams that were invisible to the naked eye.

He climbed over the fence with no problems. In the deserted gatehouse, the cable vault that served the laser network was vulnerable. If this place was true to form, he couldn't short out the lasers or disconnect them without the usual alarm being sounded. Strangely, he could not find an alarm.

The odds favored Quang being overconfident. Carter knew his electronics, and no alarm existed once the circuits were cut. Not unless some genius had designed one that was invisible or wired in at the house.

He cut the cable and checked the security pattern. He saw no lasers and heard no alarms.

The house was a hundred feet from the gatehouse. Carter kept to the shadows of a high hedge that bordered the driveway until he was in the shadows of the house itself. A figure in black, his face covered with camouflage makeup, he crept around the structure, looking in every window.

He saw no one. He heard nothing. But he was in no hurry, so he gave it a full half hour before he eased Hugo into the doorjamb at the rear of the house and slipped the lock. If a silent alarm had been sounded outside the property, someone would have responded by now.

The lower floor was deserted. It was spacious and well appointed as he expected. Two stairways led to the upper floors, one from the front hall and the other for the servants leading from the pantry at the back of the house. Carter chose the front stairs. From experience he knew that the front stairs were probably of stone, covered with carpet, while the other stairway was of wood. He wanted no creaky steps to give away his presence.

The master bedroom was the first door on the right. He eased the door open and stepped into the shadows. The two lumps in the bed were Quang and his wife, asleep. The man was of slight build, his features bland, his years indeterminate. The woman was no beauty. Her hair was in curlers and covered by an unattractive net. Her skin shone from the lotions she applied before retiring. They both slept soundly.

Carter pulled an object that looked like a pen from his pocket, one of Schmidt's gadgets. He held the tip near Quang's face and depressed the end. One small cloud of gas entered the sleeping man's nostrils, enough to ensure he'd not wake for at least an hour.

While Carter moved to the other side of the bed, the woman moved her head from the pillow and stared at him, her eyes wide with fright. He reacted instantaneously, and coverd her mouth with one hand while he administered the gas with the other. As he moved away, replacing the pen-like object, he smiled to himself at the thought of her awakening. Would it all seem like a bad dream to her or would she convince Quang that they'd had a nocturnal visitor? No matter. They'd find the severed cable in the morning in any case.

The desk in Quang's bedroom produced nothing of value. In an office next door, Carter struck gold. The overconfident successor to the prime minister kept documents at home linking him to both Chen and the Soviet Union. Carter took a few minutes to read the most incriminating. Quang was obviously playing both sides of the fence, but seemed to lean a bit in Chen's direction. The papers confirmed that the Soviet presence had been small. They were eliminated and couldn't be replaced during this action. So it was just between him and Chen now. Good. He'd take the better odds and run with them.

One set of papers was doubly intriguing. Quang had a plan on file to destroy Chen. He had a complete floor plan of Chen's fortress, including some kind of elaborate war room filled with consoles. Unfortunately, the plan didn't provide an address. Carter would still have to find that out for himself.

Pulling a small camera from a pocket, Carter reflected that Hawk would like to see the evidence, and he'd make sure Chief Windsor received prints.

He was finished in less than a minute. Eight shots were enough. They would be very dark but readable.

While he prepared to leave, his mind on the next problem—whether to tackle Quang's Market Street office—he heard a sound in the hall outside.

Carter decided his best plan was to wait, to let the other party make the first move. He made sure the doors to the small balcony outside the bedroom were ajar and stood back in the shadows.

The door opened slowly. A huge man in pajama bottoms slipped silently into the room carrying a large handgun. Carter had a problem. Was this one of Quang's personal guards, perhaps supplied by Chen? Or was the man a civil servant, one of Chief Windsor's people assigned to a high government official?

No. It couldn't be the latter, he thought. One of Chief Windsor's men would never roam the halls of this house dressed as he was. It had to be someone close to Quang. The decision made, the problem simplified itself.

Carter quietly slipped Wilhelmina from her holster under his left armpit. He held the Luger by the barrel and used the weapon as a club when the dark shadow moved within range.

Carter caught the heavy body and eased it to the floor. He'd been there long enough. It was time to get out.

While he jogged from the house to the gate, a thought kept nagging at him. Why had he seen a monitor in every room of the house he searched? Why monitors and no consoles? The viewers were neither television screens nor monitors for computers. If they were Chen's, they were strong evidence that Chen had a hold on Quang stronger than Carter had thought at first.

His weakness was his measure of the enemy. An adversary who never came out in the open ws the most dangerous of all species. You never knew his real strengths, you never knew his weaknesses. One possible weakness had occurred to him. If Chen was secluded in what could only be an electronic listening post, that fact in itself would be the man's weakness. Enemies who moved around a great deal and changed appearances were harder to stamp out.

On the other side of the coin, a man with a large enough network could have eyes everywhere. It wasn't unlike an assignment he'd had in Hong Kong when an entire enemy tong had been on the lookout for him. Ten thousand pairs of eyes made one hell of an intelligence network.

Samantha Trail wasn't accustomed to working as the junior member of a team. While Barney Feldman and she had been equals on the surface, he had deferred to her most of the time, knowing more often than not that she had a better sense of the situation than he. Carter had never made it clear that he was totally in charge, but his presence was intimidating. Maybe it was all in her head, maybe he unconsciously took charge, but whatever it was, she felt almost reluctant to make a move on her own.

She called Chief Windsor and brought herself up to date on his talks with Carter. She called Howard Schmidt and exchanged pleasant banter with him, all of which took five minutes. It was not enough. Not when Carter was out there. She roamed the room like a caged tiger, unaccustomed to inactivity, and she thought about the man who had torn down the wall that for years had deprived her of any feeling of true womanhood.

She thought about the first feel of him, the first welling up of feeling that had driven her to take advantage of him when he wasn't really in total control. And she thought about his gracious handling of the situation.

She had to do her best for him. It was a compulsion now.

She stopped pacing and moved to the bed. She spread out, legs apart, her hands behind her head. The lights were still on. She sniffed. The place smelled strange. An odor she had never smelled before seemed to engulf her. A weariness took over and her eyelids closed, not as if she were merely drowsy, but as if they had been glued closed by an unknown force.

The last thing she remembered was a feeling that dark shapes moved beside her bed, enfolded her in some kind of sling, and moved her into a conveyance. Some kind of dream. The kind she didn't need right now.

Carter decided against searching the Tuan Sing Tower, convinced he had enough on Quang to make the connection to Chen. He headed back to the River View, content for the moment.

It was still dark, just after four. He entered silently, not wanting to wake Samantha. The room was very quiet, and it smelled differently somehow, not as he'd left it. Coming out of the lighted hall to the dark room, he bumped a shin against a chair and swore. When the sound of his own voice drifted into silence, he couldn't even hear her breathing. He turned on the light on his side of the bed and saw only the imprint of her on the bedspread.

Samantha hadn't slept in the bed. She wasn't in the bathroom. He was annoyed. He'd asked her to make a couple of simple calls and wait for him. He'd requested that she not go to the embassy until much later.

Samantha was a trained agent. Even if she didn't like it, she would have followed orders. He picked up the phone and called Chief Windsor. Almost as if the man never slept, he was on the phone in less than a minute.

"Did you talk to Samantha tonight?" Carter asked.

"She called me earlier. Why?"

"When was that?"

"Two. Maybe two-thirty," Chief Windsor said, the tone of his voice revealing his concern. "Where is she, Carter? I told you to take care of her."

"She's not here. There's no sign of a struggle. She hasn't used the bed except to lie on top of it."

"Bloody hell! They've got her. How does the place smell?"

"Strange you should ask. I've never smelled anything like it."

"That's it, then. Hotel thieves brew up their own gas from a potent root. They introduce it into the keyhole of a hotel room door and rob the occupants. Any sign they carried her out?"

"No. Can your people interview the hotel staff?"

"By the time we get started they'll all be going off duty. But we'll have a go."

"If they've taken her, where do you think she is?" Carter asked.

"The House, wherever that is."

"Have your people drag in all their informants. Comb every source you have."

"You don't have to tell me, old boy. What are you going to do?"

"There's only one way to go: let them take me, and hope they'll take me to the same place."

"Watch yourself, Carter. I know you can handle yourself, but we have no guarantee they won't kill you both as soon as they lay their hands on you."

"That's part of the job, Chief Windsor. Usually they stop long enough to try one interrogation. Let's hope they run true to form."

"Right you are. I'm off to muster my people. Good luck."

Carter sat on a chair in the deserted room and thought about Samantha. Hawk would be furious. He asked himself how he felt. She was a big girl. She'd decided to be an agent without having her arm twisted and she knew the risks. But the timing was lousy.

Wearily, he picked up the phone to call Howard Schmidt. He had to know if she'd carried out his orders.

They seemed to be broken up into small groups of five or six. When they moved from one activity to another they frequently passed another group trudging along, heads down, some weeping, others like walking dead, all without hope.

They were not degraded by having to move about naked. They were not abused sexually. But they were subjected to one small torture after another.

She had lost track of time. When the gas, or whatever it was they'd used on her, had worn off, she'd been attached to a group and been forced to sit on a stool under a cold shower until the cold seeped into the core of her bones.

Her group was made up of two Orientals, a man and woman past middle age, a German businessman, a Buddhist monk, and herself. They were permitted to talk all they wanted, so she knew that she was in a place called the House and she was the prisoner of Fat Chen. From time to time she would see the image of a gargantuan Chinese on a screen as he shouted instructions at the keepers in a voice that shook the walls and hurt her ears. They told her the fat man with the gleaming dome was Fat Chen. Television cameras seemed to be mounted everywhere. They told her Fat Chen could observe their every move.

It seemed like forever, but she'd probably been there for only a few hours. From the cold shower they'd been led to a whipping room where they'd all been caned on the back and buttocks, not enough to break the skin but enough to start a fire beneath the skin that nothing would quench.

Room to room, hall to hall, an endless, mindless, ever-escalating succession of tortures. No one seemed to be in a hurry. They had found a successful formula and were sticking to it. No one asked them questions. They were being softened up, not permitted to relieve themselves or sleep until the interrogators were ready for them.

As they reached the fifth or sixth plateau of this nightmare, they were led into a room that was barren except for a bench with a kind of wooden vise attached. Samantha was last, forced to watch as each in succession had his left arm secured in the vise. This torture was selective. It was a horrible psychological Russian roulette game in which a man standing to one side nodded or shook his head as each prisoner's arm was ready for his decision.

He seemed to nod his head when they had an old or weak subject in the vise and the guards would break the subject's wrist. The sound of the bone snapping and the scream of the victim sent a cold rush of fear through those who waited their turn. Strangely, the man in charge would shake his head when the subject was strong. But not always. She couldn't be sure of the pattern.

When it was her turn, Samantha was faced with the worst ordeal since her rape. She watched the man, her eyes glued to his face, unable to look elsewhere, a small river of sweat pouring from her chin.

He nodded his head. The sound of her wrist snapping filled the dank room. When it was over, she fainted.

He was sitting on a stool under a cold shower. The last thing he remembered was dropping off to sleep and the smell in the room increasing as sleep found him. He was in a group of seven prisoners. He was the only Occidental. He didn't let them know he could speak their dialects but listened to them chatter between sessions of torture that grew in intensity as they moved from one stone room to another.

After the whipping that was almost a joke compared to the tortures he'd suffered in his life, he'd seen Samantha being dragged along with a group that looked as if they'd been through the mill. He was alert enough to note the swollen left arms of some in the group, some with the bone protruding. He had to get out of there fast and take Samantha with him. At the very least, he had to escape and set Chief Windsor's hounds on the place before they went too far with his colleague. She looked bad.

They entered another small stone room that was furnished with only a bench and a strange-looking wooden vise. He knew what it was instantly and his fears were confirmed when the first victim in his group, a little old man, was led to the vise and had his left wrist broken.

It was now or never. When it was his turn, one muscular Oriental took him by the arm and led him to the bench. Carter turned and shoved two fingers and the thumb of his right hand in the man's diaphragm, putting everything he had into it. The other guard came at him with a growl starting deep in his throat.

Carter whirled, keeping clear of the prisoners, and chopped the guards in the gut with a karate kick, using his heel as the point of contact, utilizing all the strength of his thighs. He was not in the least weakened by what had gone on before. He whirled toward the bench, picked it up, vise and all, raised it over his head, and hurled it with all his might at the cold-eyed one who seemed to be in charge.

In the earlier sessions, Carter had memorized the layout of the House. He moved from room to room, challenged by guards, fighting his way to find Samantha.

It was hopeless. She was nowhere to be found. In a last-ditch effort to do his best for her and to save his mission, he dived out a window, rolled in the grass, and took off into the woods surrounding the house.

Chief Windsor was at his desk. The man never seemed to go home.

"The House is a two-story block structure on Admiralty Road West about a half mile east of the causeway. I'll try to be out front. Move your ass on this one, Chief. I couldn't bring her out."

NINE

Carter was not pursued from the house. After finding the coin telephone a block away he'd returned to stand across the street and watch. Nothing seemed to be going on inside, no lights, no movement, nothing.

In less than five minutes the whine of double-noted sirens filled the air. The house was soon surrounded by police vehicles. Men stood or crouched behind them with every kind of small arms trained on the house. Chief Windsor stood with a knot of his best men, about to enter, when Carter joined them.

They made the usual moves as they went about the business of taking over the first floor. One man kicked in a door while two others went in low, their weapons at the ready, their task made more difficult by the presence of so many prisoners.

Nothing moved. Bodies littered the floor. Chief Windsor rolled one of the guards on his back and smelled his breath.

"Cyanide," he said, and shook his head.

"The prisoners . . . what hit them?" the police chief's lieutenant asked in wonder as he looked about him.

The prisoners were in small groups. They were all dead. Atomizers of cyanide lay beside them on the floor where the guards had dropped them.

"Looks like it was all rehearsed," Carter commented. "You have to fear something more than death to go this way."

"But where's Samantha?" Chief Windsor said tightly.

"It doesn't look good," Carter muttered.

They searched the building, evey room, every corner, looked at every body. She wasn't there. They combed the grounds until one of the officers shouted for them to come over. He stood near a ditch at the back of the building.

"Here! She's over here!"

Carter and Chief Windsor were the first on the scene, one at either side of her. Carter felt for a pulse at her throat. It was strong and steady. She opened her eyes, smiled, then passed out again. The two men looked at each other and grinned. Somehow she had made it out a window and crawled this far.

They carried her gently to a waiting ambulance. She would be the only one not transported in a body bag.

"So we don't have a single witness against Chen," Carter said, his feet up on Chief Windsor's desk, his hand curled around a cigarette as he prepared to light it.

"Same as always."

"What about all the television equipment? Does it lead us anywhere?" Carter asked.

"Futile. It was all radio-controlled, doesn't lead anywhere, nothing conclusive."

"So we're back where we were," Carter grumbled.

"Not entirely," the police chief said. "I've been after the location of that house for a long time. Chen will try to replace it, but it'll take months."

"I'll have him before that," Carter said confidently.

"Don't underestimate him, Carter. You're up against power beyond belief."

"Thanks for the warning. But don't worry, I'll watch out for myself."

"What's next for you?"

Carter took a couple of fingers of scotch that was offered and lifted his glass in a salute. "A trip to our embassy for new supplies. A trip to the hospital to see Samantha."

"I'll see her later. Say hello for me."

"Will do," he said, downing the drink and standing to leave.

"Carter," Chief Windsor said, causing the man from AXE to turn from the door. "I realize she's taken with you. Don't play games with her."

"She's a big girl, Chalkie," Carter said, using the man's nickname for the first time. "She knows where she stands with me. No games. No commitments. Nothing beyond this assignment. That's the best I can do."

"Good enough," the Britisher said. "But if you don't stick to that, I'll have your bloody ass."

Something had occurred to Carter and he'd almost forgotten it in the exchange with Windsor. "I'd like to have an autopsy report on at least two of the bodies," he suggested.

"Why? My man's up to his armpits with work. What could possibly . . . ?"

"I've got a hunch."

"What are we looking for?"

"I'm not sure. But if Chen is so entrenched in electronic listening, we might find something."

"All right. I'll have them take a look."

Carter thought about the police chief's last comment about Samantha as he drove to the embassy in the old Cortina. The battered old British Ford was his only sanctuary in the city. Chen seemed to know all the other places they'd used as they'd dropped from hotel to hotel. He probably had the hospital and the embassy watched, but Carter couldn't help that. He had to play his own game, and hiding in a hotel room wasn't going to get the work done.

He drove to the embassy first, parked the car on High Street, and called from a public telephone. He dialed and asked for their chargé d'affaires. The man, Solomon Fry, a mousy man in stature and outlook, was at his desk.

"Yes, I have your package, Carter, and I don't appreciate your using me as a messenger boy."

Carter ignored the remark. "How can I get in the embassy without being seen?"

"You can't."

"Then someone will have to deliver the package to me. I don't know anyone else in your shop, so it'll have to be you."

"Now see here, Carter, I will not take orders from an outsider—"

Carter cut him off. "I have clout you wouldn't believe, Mr. Fry. Do you want the order personally issued by the president? Is that what it's going to take?"

"Well, no . . . ."

"Meet me in the lobby of the Supreme Court Building in five minutes," he said, and hung up. He didn't like pulling rank on men like Fry. But he had a job to do. The Frys of this world lived in a cocoon and should never be in the diplomatic service. It was always a mystery to Carter that they seemed to exist everywhere.

The little man appeared on time carrying the package. Carter hung back behind a column and watched for a minute or two to make sure no one had followed the embassy man. When he strode up to Fry, the foreign service officer started to berate him for being late.

"I had to be sure you weren't being followed," Carter said, grinning. "No point in your being shot in the process."

The little man turned on his heel and scurried from the imposing lobby. The guard on duty gave Carter a quizzical look. If he'd known what was in the package, he'd have blown the whistle and come on the run, his gun in his hand.

The Killmaster walked casually down the steps of the imposing government building and made his way to the Cortina, making sure he wasn't being followed. He drove around for a half hour, again watching his back, until he was sure he was in the clear.

The hotel he picked was not far from the embassy, the Victoria, on Victoria Street, an extension of Hill Street or perhaps the other way around. It was a small hotel with many of the rooms not air-conditioned, a place he'd not be expected to use.

The room was large and airy. He opened the windows to a brisk harbor breeze and stripped down to take a shower. Later, with just a towel around his waist, he sat on the bed and opened the briefcase Schmidt had sent by army jet overnight. One man, one plane. It was the best and the fastest courier service in the world and only available because of Hawk's standing in Washington.

The small grenades were all there, at least three dozen of them. He examined one carefully, making sure he was familiar with the quick release pin and the small timer dial. With practice, a weapons expert would be able to set the timer and toss the grenades, one after the other, at about five-second intervals. He had something in mind that might take a bit longer.

The phosphorous grenades, a half dozen, were painted white to save confusion. They were without timers, so Carter assumed they were set for ten seconds. Schmidt had included the small gas bombs as requested and a large wad of Singapore bills. Carter counted fifteen one-thousand-dollar bills and estimated the rest to be worth about ten thousand Singapore dollars, more than enough. It was now time to visit the hospital.

The Mount Elizabeth Hospital, on a street bearing its name, was in the most beautifully green part of a garden-like city. The flower beds surrounding the front of the large hospital looked more like those seen in botanical gardens than in hospital landscaping. Huge old trees were everywhere. It was another tribute to Hue Yen that everyone took pride in the appearance of the city.

"Miss Trail is not registered in my files," the receptionist said after consulting her computer."

"Can you tell me who treated her and where he or she might be?" Carter asked.

"That is confidential information. Are you a relative?" the handsome middle-aged Chinese woman asked.

"I'm her lover," Carter told her, knowing the effect the statement would have on her. She would be so anxious to share her knowledge with her friends, she'd give him what he wanted just to get rid of him and be free to talk.

"Dr. Yao is the name I have. Ask for him in Emergency."

Emergency was on the street floor not far from reception. Dr. Yao was treating a patient but allowed Carter to stand by as he finished bandaging a small boy's knee.

"Miss Trail would not let us check her in," he told Carter when he was finished. "She insisted that after we got the swelling down, she be fitted with a cast and be on her way."

"But the pain . . ."

"A broken wrist can be traumatic to some but not to others. She seemed to be in control. It was a clean break, so we let her go."

"Where . . . ?" Carter started to ask, but he knew it was a stupid question to ask a busy doctor. He found a pay phone and called Chief Windsor.

"She's checked out. Has she called you?" he asked.

"No."

"I'm at the Victoria Hotel under the name Jack Clifford. If she calls you, tell her, okay?"

"I will," Windsor said. He sounded tired, as if all the fight had been drained out of him. "Perhaps she's just gone to ground for a while," he suggested.

Carter hung up feeling at a loss to know where to make contact with her. It was getting late again. The sun had gone down and the sky was clouded over. When he returned to his hotel room, discouraged, he switched on the overhead light and stood at the door, totally surprised.

She sat up in bed, pulling the covers over her breasts with one hand. "Close the door and come to bed," Samantha said casually. "I thought you'd never get back."

• • •

The glow of the green monitors reflected from the polished dome of Fat Chen as he sat in his huge chair. He looked different. The round contours of his face and body seemed to be rent with cracks as if he'd been damaged. He sat, slumped, worry lines creasing his forehead, the huge mound of flesh almost deflated like a burst balloon.

The biggest monitor in front of him, fully three feet square, showed the face of Robert Quang. He was talking, his voice taking on the tones of a frightened man, his words a plea for his own future.

"She said she saw this apparition in black. One of my guards got a glimpse of him. He said the intruder was a beast seven feet tall."

"Fools! You listen to fools!"

"But my wife—"

"A chattering woman! A stupid woman! You listen to the braying of fools, Quang!"

"How do you explain the destruction of the House?"

"He was one man. One mortal man. He was lucky. Our people were too lax."

"And what do you propose now?"

"Did he find anything incriminating at your house?" Chen demanded.

"I'm not a fool. I keep nothing incriminating at my house," Quang lied. He had looked over his papers but could not be sure they had not been tampered with. On the other hand, he could not be sure they had not been duplicated in some way. He was past the point of worry. He was frantic. If Chen found out the truth, he was a dead man.

"I don't understand why the man, whoever he is, didn't search your office," the huge Chinese spoke to the screen. "He had the freedom of your house and you say he found nothing. Why then not search your office?"

"Your people picked him up before he had the time. I have doubled the security at my office."

"You will do better than that. You will destroy all papers connecting us."

"As you wish. What about the house? Could he have found anything incriminating there?"

"I'm not a fool like you, Quang. Nothing can be traced back to me. Nothing. Every prisoner was killed. Every guard followed his orders. Not one mouth can utter a word against me."

"But he's still out there," Quang said, his fear obvious.

"Yes. He's still out there," the monster admitted. "The next time we get our hands on him, I want him dead."

"It will be done, Excellency," Quang said, his voice almost a whine.

"But I want him interrogated first. I have to know who he is and who sent him. I want no repeats of what this man has done. It is bad for morale."

"Every eye in Singapore is on him," Quang said, trying to sound bolder than he felt. "We will have him soon."

Chen moved a pudgy hand to cut off the communication. Beside his right hand a master switch had been installed to cut off all power to his monitors and consoles. In the years since he'd isolated himself, he had never used the switch. He used it now.

The green glow of the room slowly faded. Residual light from cathode ray tubes continued to paint the huge man a faint greenish tinge for long moments after he had thrown the switch.

He sat, totally immobile, a hungry predator in the dark, out of his element.

He had to *think*. All the monitors and all the cameras he had scattered around the city were of no use. The thousands of eyes that served him were of no use. For the first time in his adult life he doubted himself.

He had seen the man on his monitor when they had him at the House. He had observed his cold acceptance of the process of softening up prisoners. He had even seen the man grasp his opportunity and escape. He had not seemed superhuman. But he had not seemed vulnerable, even when in the hands of his people at the House.

Who was he? What was he? How could he, one insignificant man, bring the Chen organization to a complete standstill?

And what was he doing right now?

He sat in the unaccustomed darkness and tried to find a solution, tried to analyze his own weaknesses.

His body heat dropped. He started to shiver. The chair that held him began to creak under his weight as great sobs shook him.

After a few minutes of self-pity, he shook himself, firmed up his shoulders, sat up straighter in the chair, and flipped on the master switch.

The green glow grew stronger as images began to appear on activated screens. The fresh glow illuminated a more resolute man. His face was as inscrutable as the round dome permitted. What had he to fear? Was he not the power to be feared? He switched his consoles to show the constant pattern of his robots outside and he swelled with pride at his own power and brilliance.

One man. One poor, weak, mortal man.

Let him come. He would be destroyed.

All the questions that boiled up in Carter's head were put aside as he stood by the door for a moment just looking at her. The deep brown eyes stared at him, crinkled in a smile. The long oval face was shadowed beneath the cheekbones, the dark smudges adding to the beauty of her. She was wearing a peach-colored turban to cover her shaved head.

Samantha slowly pulled the sheet aside with one hand and held her arms out to him.

Carter flipped off the light, and the room was cast in a rosy glow from the lights outside. He walked over to the bed. Her skin was hot to the touch. She moaned as he ran his hands over her, then set about the task of pulling off his shirt, her hands frantic for the touch of him.

He lay with her a long time, his mouth on hers until her insistence and the urgency of his need drove them to cast off the rest of his clothing and come together.

Once again, it seemed incredible to Carter that he had ever thought this body to be a man's. She opened herself to him, a beautiful flower, and guided him with an urgency that spoke of her recent awakening. This would be the first time she had been with a man with no trepidation from the first moment and at her instigation. She seemed to glow with the anticipation of sensations that had been new to her until only very recently.

Carter was in no hurry. Life passed by all too quickly and showed its ugly side all too often. Moments like these were to be taken slowly and savored like fine wine.

Samantha's attitude was quite different. She could wait no longer for the ecstasy she had experienced with this man. The depths of her seemed like an open flame as she brought them together. He paused momentarily to suck in his breath before expelling it in one long sigh, a sound that caused her to become still more demanding.

He could see that he could not slow the pace—not this first time tonight. He moved over and into her, felt himself rising to a peak more quickly than he would have liked, but rejoiced at the result it created in her.

Samantha was in the midst of one long orgasm. He held himself back, waiting for her passion to wane. But it did not. It went on for what seemed like minutes, the heat of her breath on his neck, the cries of her pleasure sharp and unmistakable in their joy.

Carter took her cries as a signal to add to her excitement. He let himself go. The psychological effect on her was startling. The fact that she had given him pleasure seemed to take her over the top, to add to her own pleasure, almost to the point of pain.

Then it was over. Her breath came in ragged gulps as she clung to him, repeating his name over and over, almost like a chant.

"Oh, Nick. I'll never in my life feel anything approaching that. My God! I owe you so much."

He moved slowly off her, caressing her still, basking in the afterglow of the pleasure she had given him. "Not so, my sweet Sam. It was there all the time, hungry to get out." His breath, too, was ragged. Even in the superb physical condition that he maintained, the energy she had demanded had taken its toll. "We'll be together again. You will love other men. Think of it as a beginning."

"It will never be like this," she said, holding him tight, tears rolling down her cheeks.

"I won't argue. But you'll see," he said as he released her and rolled to his back. "How did you find me?" he asked her at last. "I thought I'd covered my tracks."

She lay on her back, her breasts flat to her chest as it heaved with the last of her deep breaths. "Chen is not the only one here with an organization. I was lucky. One of my people is a porter here."

"Good. I was afraid I'd slipped up somewhere. Fat Chen seems to have eyes everywhere."

"Are we going to stay here? I have a couple of safe houses we could use."

"They may be useful yet. It does seem like we've been doing a lot of hotel hopping," he said. "But that's all over, I hope."

"Why? What's changed?"

"As far as I'm concerned, Chen is the power behind all the action here. Hawk was very specific: find and destroy whoever is behind the trouble here."

"But we haven't found him."

"We've accomplished a lot," he said, reaching for his cigarettes and lighter. He lit two and handed one to her. "The Russians are out of it. I've found proof that Robert Quang is up to his neck in it. As you say, we have to find Chen. He's the real monster. When we do, I'll destroy him."

She put her cigarette in an ashtray and snuggled closer. "I wish I could be as confident as you. The man is the most powerful crime lord in the Far East. He controls all of Malaysia. What about his mansion? I've heard it's impregnable."

"Nothing is impregnable," he said, putting one arm around her, permitting her to curl up even closer. "Chen, like every overconfident megalomaniac before him, will have chinks in his armor. I've already got some ideas as to how we'll destroy him."

"Let's forget about Chen," Samantha said, moving against Carter, her skin hot, her breath starting to come in little gasps again.

He crushed out his cigarette and held her close. She was content for a moment or two, then slipped from his arms and gracefully straddled his thighs. "I've wanted to do this from the first time you touched me," she whispered. "Relax and leave the action to me."

Carter was not about to argue. He was many things but he was not a fool.

Chief Windsor stood by the coroner and looked down at the body. "What is it?" he asked.

"An implant. Don't ask me exactly what," the coroner said.

"I'm into electronics as a hobby," one of the other medical examiners ventured. "It looks like a small transmitter to me."

Chief Windsor needed no confirmation. Of course it would be a transmitter. "You found one on the other dead man?" he asked.

"The same."

"Thanks for taking the time. It payed off," Windsor said as he turned from the table.

As he let himself out of the white-tiled room, his active brain was trying to sort out the facts. What the hell was he dealing with here? Chen was known to have video cameras in hundreds of key locations. But to implant listening devices in his guards? The man had to be totally paranoid. He'd have to have equipment to tune in on all his people, hundreds or even thousands of frequencies, something beyond the range of normal technology. His people would have to be so afraid of him, they'd subject themselves to anything to serve him. It confirmed the awesome reality of the cyanide deaths. This man had to be the ultimate, the most ruthless criminal he'd ever dealt with.

The listening devices helped form a pattern, but the evidence would never convict Chen of anything. They had yet to tie him in to a specific crime.

He thought about Nick Carter. In all of his career he'd never run into anyone like him. He'd also never given a man so much latitude. But what else could he do? Chen and Quang had to be stopped and doing it himself was impossible. He wondered where Carter was now and what he was doing.

TEN

Samantha was lying on her left side, the arm with the cast stretched out before her. She looked beautiful and very vulnerable. A feeling of tenderness welled up in Carter and he decided the next act in the drama would be a solo.

He shook her gently. She opened her eyes and smiled up at him, instant recognition and love flooding her face.

"Hi," she said, stretching sleepily. "You're all dressed. Where are you going?"

"I don't want you in on this until you're feeling stronger."

"Where are you going?" she repeated, her smile turning into a frown.

"Looking for Chen. He owns three estates, right? You said he had one on Telok Blangah Road near the Ginseng Essence Balm Park, one on Pioneer Road near the Jurong Bird Park, and one on Lady Hill Road."

"Not without me, buster."

"I don't want to pull rank, Sam. I just want you to stay put for another day or two," he said, sitting on the bed beside her. "You're an experienced agent. I'm not going to coddle you. Just give it another couple of days, okay?"

"All right. But I suggest we get out of here. What about one of my safe houses? They're not much for comfort, but they're safer than a hotel now. I should have taken you to one earlier."

"Maybe you're right. Where?"

"I've got two. The best equipped is on Pekin Street in Chinatown, number Thirty-seven. It's a gift shop in front. Just pass through the bead curtains at the back and ask for me."

"Sounds good. I'm getting weary of all this moving around from hotel to hotel. But I've got one errand for you before we're done with the hotels. Can you get into my suite at the Shangri-la and pick something up?"

Samantha smiled broadly. "The housekeeper is the second cousin of one of my best people."

"In a clothes closet she'll find a cesta. Take it to the safe house. And take this case." He indicated the briefcase Schmidt had just sent over. "We'll probably need it."

"Just one question: What the hell's a cesta?"

"He laughed as he moved to the door. "It's a wicker throwing device, a kind of curved basket used in jai alai. You know what I mean?"

"I've seen them, sure, but I never knew what they were called. Okay. But I'm beginning to wonder about you, Carter," she said, a puzzled expression on her face. "The famous Killmaster wants me to pick up a toy for him. Is it okay if I ask why?"

"It's all part of my fiendish plot, lovely lady spy," he said with an evil cackle as he reached for the door. Then he added seriously, "Take care of yourself. "I'll see you at the safe house."

It was dark by the time he drove the Cortina along Orange Grove Road near the Lady Hill mansion. Instead of watching his back, he was thinking about Samantha, and his mind was also going over the floor plans for the Chen fortress he'd found in Quang's house, remembering every detail. It was going to be one hell of a tough nut to crack. But first he had to find it.

Before he reached any of Chen's addresses, some of his people came at Carter in two cars. One was a tanklike replica of a Checker cab, the other an old Buick Electra. Either car outweighed his Cortina two to one.

They had clubs, obviously intent on taking him alive.

Carter was fully armed. Before he'd left, he'd slipped on his weapons. He never liked eight-to-one odds, but fully armed, he'd fought his way out of worse situations.

They didn't come at him in any predetermined formation, just piled out of the cars and moved as quickly as they could.

Carter was out and firing faster than they could get to him. He caught the nearest two in the head. They fell backward into their own people, blood, bone chips, and brain matter spraying them all.

In the second or two of respite, Carter used two of his 9mm bullets to take out a tire on each car, an act that might provide insurance if he got past the wall of flailing clubs.

One club—they were like slim baseball bats—clipped his gun hand and sent Wilhelmina flying. Hugo was in his right palm in an instant and creased the next two who got within range.

While they backed off slightly, two dead and two

slashed badly, one moved in on him from the rear, his crepe-soled shoes silent.

Carter's ear was atuned to the slightest sound. He waited until the perfect moment and swung to the side, catching the club in the palm of his left hand and wresting it from his attacker as it swung on him.

Armed with his stiletto in one hand and the club in the other, the odds were beginning to feel much better. One man came at him in a frontal attack, his club arcing at the man from AXE menacingly.

Carter ducked under the club, paralyzed the man's hand with a blow to the knuckles, and skewered him on the needle-sharp blade.

The short encounter had taken too long. Too late, Carter sensed one of the clubs moving through the air at his back. While he turned to ward off the blow, the club crashed against his skull not an inch from the still tender lump he'd received only days ago.

Strangely it didn't hurt, but he felt his knees buckle. The last thing he remembered was the whine of a familiar double-noted siren in the distance. Instead of growing louder it faded as a blanket of black swirling clouds engulfed him.

Chief Windsor stepped from the police car as it skidded to a halt. The sight that met him was straight out of a gangster movie. Two big black cars hemmed in the Cortina. Two men were dead, the back of their heads blown off. Two others couldn't see for the blood coursing from knife wounds on their scalps. One man lay moaning, a broken club next to his prostrate body, a knife wound in his chest.

"Get a line on these three vehicles," he ordered a lieutenant.

"The Cortina was driven by your American the last time we saw him," he was told.

Chief Windsor looked like a beaten man as he searched the scene with care. He found Carter's gun and his knife on the sidewalk near the dead men. Five men on the sidewalk and Carter missing. The police chief cursed under his breath. They had Carter, and he had no idea where they could have taken him. It could be any of a thousand places.

"I want the two bodies autopsied right away," he ordered. "Tell the coroner to look for electronic implants." His face was lined. He looked ten years older than the man Carter had met only days earlier. "Get the three wounded men to Emergency and keep a whole squad on guard at the hospital. If they have implants, have them removed and destroyed. I'll want to talk to them when they've recovered."

"This one won't be able to talk for a long time," one of Windsor's men offered. "He's got a soft spot on his skull the size of an orange, and a knife wound in his chest. He's in bad shape."

The police chief wasted no time on sympathy. It looked like they'd gone after Carter with a small army. God! Bloody hell! It had to be Chen, or Quang working for Chen, he thought. After seeing the evidence from Quang's desk, maybe it was Quang working alone and in the process of a takeover.

What could he do? he asked himself in frustration. His hands were tied. Robert Quang was still the second most powerful political figure in the city and they had no evidence strong enough to present to Hue Yen. Even the papers in Quang's desk didn't implicate him conclusively.

The facts could be twisted by clever argument.

He held the 9mm Luger in his hand and hefted it before he shoved it into a pocket. "I'll be in my office if anyone wants me," he told his aide. He walked to his car, his shoulders stooped.

In the car he picked up the receiver and called dispatch. "Patch me in to the Victoria Hotel," he commanded.

He waited for a full two minutes for the connection and talked with the front desk. Samantha had checked out. The room was clean of any signs of the two of them. He slumped back in his seat. Did the bloody monster have both of them?

Gradually Carter could feel his senses return, but everything was still black. He was tied to a steel chair and the chair seemed to be bolted to the floor. He was stripped to the waist, his feet bare.

He felt around the floor near the chair with his feet as night vision started to give him a glimmer of his surroundings. His feet read the pattern of the floor. It was steel. Rivet heads dotted the area around him. The whole area rocked slightly.

A ship. He was in the hold of a ship. He called out and the sound bounced back at him from four steel walls. He could see better now, but he saw nothing significant. The place was totally empty. It was large. Perhaps a hundred feet long by seventy wide. It was also a long way to the steel cover over his head. He strained to see above him and could make out a half-dozen shaded electric bulbs set in the ceiling and a large square opening that had been covered by a sliding panel.

So it was a hold. His deduction was confirmed as the

boat rocked more than before, perhaps from the wake of a passing ship.

He could hear no engine throb and could feel no forward motion. An anchor chain chafed, steel-on-steel, from time to time. They were at anchor, probably in Singapore harbor.

Carter rubbed his chin against a shoulder. He felt no appreciable beard. He'd shaved just before leaving the Victoria, so he hadn't been unconscious for long.

All his deductions led him nowhere. It didn't matter. He had to keep his brain active, to assimilate as much knowledge as he could. He'd been taken by enemies before and it was always some bit of information he'd gleaned from observation of a small mistake by the enemy that had saved him.

His mental exercises were interrupted before he'd gone very far. The overhead lights flashed on, almost blinding him, and a bulkhead was thrown open, clanging against the hull. A line of men walked toward him. Robert Quang was the fourth man to come into view. He was dressed as he might for a session in Parliament or an interview with his boss Hue Yen. Carter had seen Quang in bed, vulnerable, his hair rumpled, his mouth agape as he slept. They were two different men. This one carried an air of command—and one other thing. His face had the unmistakable look of a man with a mission, prepared to be as ruthless as the task required.

Carter was distracted for a moment as two men came in from another bulkhead pushing a cart and trailing a set of cables. A video monitor. It had a camera installed over the cathode ray tube. He should have known Chen wouldn't be left out of this. It tied the two men together conclusively, but that information wasn't going to do Carter any good unless he survived.

"You defiled my house," Quang spat at Carter while the men set up the monitor.

"And I doubt your friend Chen knows what I found," he shot back.

"Don't activate the monitor," Quang shouted to his men. "Chen can wait a few minutes.

"Just who are you, Carter? Who do you work for? What the hell do you want?"

"I'm a man who loves freedom," Carter said calmly. "For everyone," he added.

"Just what's that supposed to mean?"

"Let's not play games," Carter said. "You're playing both ends of this one and you'll get burned very badly. The Soviets don't forgive lightly. They've probably already sent out a team to interrogate you."

"Silence him!" Quang yelled at his men.

A muscular Chinese guard whirled a rubber hose over his head and brought it down sideways across Carter's left cheek. The pain felt like the blast of fire from a blowtorch.

"Have you heard of the Serbsky Institute, Quang? They have new drugs—"

The hose lashed at him from the other side, knocking his head to one side, stinging like fire and straining the muscles of his neck. Blood ran from both cheeks to his neck and down his bare chest.

"If Chen finds out about your selling out to the Russians, you're a dead man," Carter taunted. He could take the pain. Wounds would heal. Quang would not kill him unless he could be sure Carter hadn't passed on what he knew. It bought time and time bought opportunity.

"Who are you working with?" Quang screamed at him.

His face was distorted by hate. He seemed to have lost control.

The man was a fool. Any third-rate detective would have found by now that he was working with Samantha and Chief Windsor. How Quang had managed to get so far was a mystery. Hue Yen had to be using him as a weak substitute and had no thought of a successor. Chen had to have played with this one like a cat with a mouse. The Russians were using a malleable man already in power. It was obvious now who was the real villain. He would get Chen, but first he had to get out of this.

On a signal from Quang, one of the guards put on a black leather glove and smashed Carter in the face with a rock-hard fist. The cartilage of his nose broke. Blood poured in a steady stream down his chest.

"Who do you work for? Who knows what you have learned?" Quang shouted, his voice an octave higher.

"Go to hell, Quang," Carter muttered through the blood.

Quang nodded to his men and two of them smashed their fists into Carter's face until his lips were split and he was unable to talk.

Light glowed from the monitor as one of the men connected the cable.

"Who told you . . . ?" Quang started to say before he realized that Chen could be listening already. He had no knowledge of the implants. Chen had not been connected by monitor, but his ears had been glued to the speaker that told him all that had gone before.

"You are a fool, Quang," the gargoyle of a face glowered at him. "The man is senseless and you have learned nothing."

"How did you . . . ?"

"I can see for myself. The look of frustration on your

face tells me. The man took a beating and told you nothing. You are a weak fool and I ask myself if you can possibly serve me further."

The statement was followed by a long silence. Carter's eyes were closed but he was conscious of every word. The beating he had taken had changed his appearance but had not sapped his strength. His enemies were at each other's throats. The odds were changing.

"You still have some minor value, Quang. If anything happened to Hue Yen, you would be an asset. So you still have your life—for now," the voice from the domelike skull roared out of the monitor. "Now take this one to the interrogation room I had installed on the quarterdeck. Use the drug expert I sent you. And don't screw it up this time."

The image faded as Chen tuned them out.

"Untie him," Quang squeaked, his voice almost paralyzed by fright. "Take him to the quarterdeck. And don't make any mistakes."

Carter could see well enough through his shattered face. Four guards surrounded him after he was untied, each carrying an automatic rifle.

They marched him through a bulkhead and toward a long, narrow set of steel steps. Two guards preceded him and two brought up the rear, their submachine guns held across their chests. They were like four robots, programmed, mindless, and unbending.

Carter timed their ascent until they were close to the top, then lashed out with a karate kick that sent two of the guards tumbling down behind him. The third guard turned, his rifle describing an arc that was about to take Carter's head off.

The Killmaster ducked and used the man's momentum

to grab his gun and lever him over the rail and to the deck below. While the screams of the falling guard still filled the great steel hold, Carter swung the butt of the rifle up and into the groin of the fourth man.

The last man between him and the top of the steps dropped his gun, a look of surprise and horror transforming the normally bovine face. He fell toward Carter who bent and rolled the man over his back and down the stairs to knock down the two who were starting to recover.

The Killmaster was up and on the quarterdeck in seconds. Two men came at him. They were too close to fire without hitting each other, so they swung on him with the wooden stocks of their weapons. Carter ducked under the attack. The rifle butt of one man struck the collarbone of the other. The noise was like the snap of a dry tree limb as it bounced off the bulkhead walls.

Carter was too busy to notice the sound of the bone breaking or the grunt of the other guard as he turned to face the man with the shattered face. The open stairwell was behind the guard. One well-aimed uppercut lifted him off his feet and down the steel steps.

Even Carter's exceptional physical conditioning was taxed by the beating and the fight. He had his strength, but he was still not free. He raced on bare feet to the short flight of stairs leading to the night air and was on the open deck in seconds.

A guard fired from the poop deck, the small missiles from his gun sending sparks into the blackness near Carter.

Dressed in the tattered remnants of his pants, he didn't hesitate. He raced for the rail and dived in a long, clean arc until he hit the water, piercing the surface with Olympic precision, hardly creating a splash.

He'd soared through the air for a long time. The depth

of his plunge surprised him. Had he landed parallel to the surface, it would have been like falling onto concrete from a ten-story building.

The water felt cool and soothing to his bruised skin. It was an element that was familiar to him. He was in no hurry. Men would be at the rail of the ship waiting to fire on him when he surfaced.

A practiced swimmer can cover a lot of distance in four minutes, and Carter intended to stay submerged to his limit. He came up far enough away from the ship to avoid detection. The men on the rail seemed a long way off.

He looked around in the light chop of the harbor as he continued to tread water. He was surrounded by enormous freighters. It would be easy to swim to the third or fourth one removed from his enemies and hail the watch for help.

But Chen owned a large percentage of the fleet. It would be like playing Russian roulette. The harbor lights were about four miles away. He could make it if he paced himself. He started out in a steady distance-eating crawl to the shore.

ELEVEN

Carter was tempted to wade ashore at Sentosa Island and catch his breath, but he wasn't known there. To wade ashore, a half-naked derelict with a damaged face, would invite too much curiosity, something that could play into the hands of Chen's people. Besides, he knew a shopkeeper near the Empire dock, a man of discretion whom he had helped in the past.

The Empire dock was quiet at that time of night. Chen's guards had taken his Rolex, but he knew it had to be past midnight. He pulled himself up a slippery vertical ladder to the dock and sat, winded, waiting to regain his full strength and to evaluate his surroundings.

Wan Foo's place was less than a block away. He glided through the shadows and confronted the old man who was sitting alone in a back room smoking a pipe.

They greeted each other formally in Mandarin. The old man disregarded his friend's condition while Carter ignored the fact that his old friend was almost in a state of trance from the opium.

"I have need of your telephone, old father," Carter said.

"My house is at your disposal," Wan Foo responded, still with all the formality and dignity of a regal meeting.

Carter called Chief Windsor and brought him up to date. He was reluctant to use the policeman, but he didn't have the number of Samantha's safe house.

"We've been frantic about you, old boy," Windsor said.

"We?" You've seen Samantha?"

"She has few secrets from me, Carter. I know where she is."

"Then you can take me there," he said, telling the police chief to pick him up in front of the Empire dock.

"May your family prosper for a thousand years," Carter said as he stood to leave.

"My house is always at your disposal, old friend Nick."

Wan Foo was far gone with opium but not that far gone that he didn't recognize Carter behind the swollen face. Friends like Wan Foo had saved Carter's life throughout his career.

The police car glided to a quiet stop and Carter crept out of the shadows to step inside.

"Pekin Street," Chief Windsor ordered his driver, a young giant who acted as the police chief's personal bodyguard.

"They'll be combing the streets for you now more than ever," Chief Windsor said, grimacing at the sight of Carter's face.

"Let them. They're shook up now, not thinking as rationally as before," Carter said, then added: "What do you think of Robert Quang?"

"He couldn't have come as far as he has without being a

winner. I don't know him personally, but he's reputed to be a strong man, bound to go a long way."

"Wrong. Sorry to disagree, Chief, but you've been misinformed," Carter said, sitting back in the car. "Do you have a cigarette."

"Sorry, no."

The driver handed back a crumpled pack of Players and a box of matches. Carter lit up and held the cigarette gingerly between smashed lips. He drew the smoke deep into his lungs and felt his ragged nerves calm.

"On what do you base your theory?" Chief Windsor asked.

"Not a theory. I've seen him, goaded him, saw him go to pieces," Carter said. "He's been a man in the right place at the right time. Chen picked him up as a front and helped build his image. He's paranoid with fear of Chen. And he was a perfect vessel for the Soviet campaign, so they moved in too."

"But he was smart enough to play both sides."

"And stupid enough to think he could play them both off and get away with it. No. He's the weak link and I'm going after him. He could be my ticket to Chen's lair."

"Good luck," Chief Windsor said as they pulled up at 37 Pekin Street. The door was opened by a frightened Chinese woman. The police chief didn't acknowledge her but moved through the bead curtains to the back.

Samantha saw Carter and Chief Windsor and jumped up from where she was sitting. She ran over to them, staring at Carter's face in horror.

"Your poor face," she murmured, pulling him into the light. "I'll get some antiseptic and bandages."

"Don't worry about it. I'll be okay," Carter said.

"But I—"

"No time. Quang was the one who took me and now we know he's the key to get at Chen. I'm going after him."

"Not alone. Not in that condition," she protested, trying to take his face in her hands.

He gently pulled her arms away. "We've got lots of business left to do tonight. Forget about my face."

She eased herself away from him, hurt.

"Do you have some clothes I could wear he asked her.

"Yes." Her answer was terse.

"And I'll need weapons. I lost mine when they took me."

"My driver has them," Windsor said. "We found them near the cars on Orange Grove Road."

"Good. I don't want to waste any time."

"What makes you think Quang will have left the ship? By the way, could you identify the ship?" the police chief asked.

"He's crossed Chen and he knows that Chen knows it. I think Chen's going to play it cool and still use Quang but no way is Quang going to stay on board when he can be safe in his own house."

"And the other question?"

"No. It was one of hundreds. It was dark. The name of the ship was obscured."

"I don't like you going to Quang's alone," Samantha said, coming out of her snit and getting into the conversation.

"You can help, but only as a lookout. I'm going to bring him out and question him here."

"I've got reports of men patrolling his grounds and house," Chief Windsor said. "Remember Carter, he's a government leader. Public sympathy's on his side."

"That may be your problem but it's not mine," Carter

said. "I'm cleaning this up for you. You've got to make some sacrifices."

"Like picking up the bodies. You seem to leave a trail after you, Carter."

"And the worst is yet to come. When we get around to Chen, it will probably sound like all-out war. You're going to have to hold off your men no matter what."

"For how long?"

"How long does a war take? Maybe ten minutes. Maybe half an hour. It could be a standoff for an hour or more."

"What about tonight?" the police chief said, the strain he'd been under showing on his face.

"Samantha will be parked just down the street. You park half a block away from her. When you see me come out with Quang, move in and clean up as quickly as possible."

"Is this going to be a war too?"

"A very silent one. When you go in, leave the cleanup to your men and you go after any records he's left there."

"Not after your first visit, surely."

"Once a stupid man, always a stupid man," Carter said. "He probably thinks lightning can't strike twice in the same place. He's just simple enough to have them all there as before."

"How will you keep this visit quiet?" Samantha asked. "George says Quang has surrounded himself with body-guards."

"Men like the ones he's hired never see a rocking chair, Sam. They know the risks. If Chief Windsor wants it quiet, it will be quiet as the grave."

"You sound like you enjoy this, Carter," the police chief accused.

Carter drew in smoke from one of his own custom-blended cigarettes. He looked from one to the other, from the sweet face of the woman who understood his life to the hardened face of a man who had seen it all but was still trying to understand. "You misread me, Chalkie," he said, talking softly with emotion. "Killing sickens me. But the moment the innocent are deprived of men like me, the world will crawl with vermin that will devour honor and decency. No, I don't like killing, but I'll kill if it advances our chances of staying civilized."

Ardmore Park was as quiet as a tomb at four in the morning. Carter got out of the car and headed for the wall of the estate. He normally wouldn't have permitted Samantha to help, but he needed transport to take Quang out and he knew that Chief Windsor would have an eye on her.

He shook himself mentally, forcing himself to maintain the icy calm and total concentration the job required. He had promised Chief Windsor a quiet war. All he had to do was get past all lasers, silence all the guards, and take Quang out by force. *I shouldn't make promises like this,* he thought. Without using Wilhelmina he might be totally out of luck.

Carter dropped to the ground inside the stone wall knowing no laser beams came within three feet of the wall. He wore goggles that detected the rays and he carried a small hand mirror. But he wasn't completely confident of the method he'd devised to get around the beams. In breaking the beam, he might trigger an alarm. What was worse, the alarm could be silent, a small warning bulb that showed up on a security monitoring board indoors.

"But there was no way to back off now. He curled the first beam to the sky and stepped past it as if he'd just swung a gate open and closed. He waited a full twenty minutes but nothing happened. The odds favored him slightly more now, but the men inside might just be a little better than average. They might be playing possum. He had no way of knowing.

There was no point in delaying now. He manipulated the beams like an expert, bending each in turn toward the heavens to allow him passage and was soon in the shadows close to the front door. The goggles showed no more beams between him and the house. He put them and the mirror in an oversize hip pocket and crept from window to window looking for the guards.

Only one room was occupied. Two guards sat in a monitoring room, playing cards, paying scant attention to the monitoring screens. With the rest of the house dark, were the others asleep or standing guard in the dark? The odds favored two on duty and two asleep, if Chief Windsor's intelligence was right, but he couldn't be sure. Quang may have beefed up the staff to twice that number.

Hugo filled his right hand at the flick of a wrist. He opened the pantry door easily with the help of the knife. The pantry and the kitchen were quiet. A night light provided a slight glow on a far wall.

The large dining room was empty. He hadn't really expected trouble in that area. There were three other rooms on the ground floor. The library was empty as was the huge living room.

Light shone below the security room off the front hall. It was obviously a converted walk-in closet. Carter eased the door open quietly, noted the two men, and closed the door again.

Question: Could he take the rest of the guards silently without warning these two, then subdue Quang and carry him out? Too much of a gamble. He ripped Pierre from his inner thigh, working too quickly, taking skin and hair with the tape.

He eased the door open a crack, twisted the two halves of Pierre, and tossed the bomb inside.

The two men saw him at the last minute. Their reaction was too slow to save themselves, but enough to knock over their chairs and make a racket as they fell across the table.

A guard came on the run, his feet encased in untied tennis shoes. He opened the door, the light flooding out into the hall. Carter cold-cocked him with the butt of his Luger and caught him as he fell. He closed the door, shutting off the light. The two who had been gassed would be out for a couple of hours. The other was good for at least a half hour.

Three down. Perhaps only one to go.

Carter padded silently up the stairs in the direction the third man had come from. Unlike the other two, he was without a coat. He'd probably been napping when he heard the noise.

In the master bedroom, Carter found Quang and his wife asleep, guarded by a man who sat snoring just inside their door. He used a paralysis hold at the base of the man's neck, then gave him a small shot of the green liquid from Schmidt's small leather case.

The master of the house and his wife slept on. Carter prowled the third floor looking for domestic help. He found evidence that they'd been there recently, but they were not there now.

So it was over. All he had to do was render Quang unconscious and carry him out.

While he was preparing a syringe with green fluid, something came at him out of the darkness in a karate leap, and a foot crashed against his ribs, knocking the syringe to the floor.

The blow felt like a ten-pound hammer swung at full force. He turned to see a small woman in jade-green silk pajamas, her head a mass of oversize rollers in a pink net. The woman was in a fighting pose that had all the style of a black-belt champion. Carter moved swiftly to take up a similar position facing her.

Quang sat up in bed, terrified, his eyes glued to the battle.

Carter feinted to the right and brought his left foot into play, catching the woman off guard, bouncing her off the far wall. The blow was from an expert, and as she picked herself up, the woman seemed to know it.

She circled cautiously, concentrating on her opponent, too wraped up in the fight to call out to her husband to run.

From what Carter could see, the woman's body was a perfect example of the female body builder but more supple and quick. Her thrusts were fast and deadly. If Carter had not been her superior in technique, he could have lost it all right there.

She came at him again and he grabbed her foot in mid-kick. He twisted, controlled her movement toward him, turned her around, and ran her into the wall. Before attending to her husband who seemed paralyzed as he sat in bed, he examined her. She was not badly hurt, just out of action for few minutes.

Carter found the small case on the floor and the syringe with the green liquid ready to inject. He cleared the needle of air, jammed it into Quang, and hoisted the small man onto his shoulders.

The ride back to the safe house was uneventful. Carter carried Quang in a back door, following Samantha.

"Where's Chief Windsor?" Carter asked as he cleared off a packing table with the sweep of one arm and stretched Quang out on his back.

"He had to get back to business. He said we should call when we're ready to work on Quang."

"This is one time we're not going to wait for him," Carter said. "From here on, if we get what I'm looking for from Quang, we're going to move fast and finish this off."

"And I'm a part of it?"

"I'm going to need you, yes."

He looked at her briefly as he pulled the small leather case from his pocket. She was excited. Maybe she wouldn't be so happy about being part of the final show-down when the firing started, but it couldn't be helped. She was a trained agent and he had a job for her.

He opened the case and withdrew a fresh syringe. He filled it with the orange liquid. It was a truth serum that Howard Schmidt had helped develop in conjunction with some biochemists from the National Research Council. It was much more reliable than what the Soviets had developed and used all too often at Serbsky. This version was more reliable than the Soviets', but it was still potentially dangerous. Where theirs could fry a brain if misused, the American version put a strain on the heart that a weak organ could not tolerate.

"I've got something for you to do while I'm working on Quang."

"But I want to be here."

"This is important. I'm not going to start for a few minutes and you could do the task in that time."

"What is it?"

"I want you to use your contacts to make two shields, oblong in shape, about four feet long by three feet wide.

They have to be made from two materials," Carter said, setting aside the syringe and lighting a cigarette. He was still all in black, his battered face covered with black makeup over a layer of lotion that protected his lacerations. He blew smoke to the ceiling away from her. The room was small and smelled of packing material. It would go up like a torch if anyone was careless with fire.

"What are they for?"

"I'll explain later. The two materials have to be glass mirror and half-inch-thick Lexan."

"The bulletproof material they use on popemobiles?"

"Exactly. The mirror will be closest to the hand and handle; the Lexan laminated to it will face an attacker."

"It sounds as if we're going into battle for sure."

"Sounds like it. Get busy, okay? I'm going to start on him when the other drug wears off. That should be in ten to fifteen minutes."

She was about to leave when he thought of an important detail. "Do you have a tape recorder here?"

"A small boom box. It's not the best, but it records," she said, plugging in the tape player and inserting a fresh tape. "Push PLAY and RECORD, same as with most of them." Samantha blew him a kiss and was out the door.

When Quang started to moan and open his eyes, Carter carefully put out his cigarette and tied one of the Oriental's wrists. He brought the shipping cord around the table, and tied the other wrist firmly. He did the same with the man's ankles.

"Where . . .? What . . .?"

The tables are reversed, Quang, old man," Carter whispered in his ear. He had pulled up a stool and sat close to the man's head. He turned on the tape recorder.

Quang was small compared to Carter, but size wasn't

the criteria. This wasn't a boxing match where the key word was "match." Quang had played the spy game both ends against the middle and this was payoff time. Carter squeezed the syringe to release a few drops, then sought a vein on the inside of Quang's arm near his elbow. He inserted the needle and gauged the dose to fit the man's body weight.

Quang didn't move but he narrowed his eyes and glared at Carter with hatred. "What's in the syringe?"

"Don't give it a thought, old man," Carter said, imitating Quang's British accent. "You'll be feeling drowsy again, but this time you won't go to sleep. Just a few questions and I'm not using a rubber hose or fists. More humane, don't you think?"

"You violated my home! My wife! What have you done with my wife?" His voice was slurred, some of the words a little indistinct.

"She's sound asleep in her own bedroom. Don't worry," Carter said. "The one we have to worry about is Arthur Cecil Chen. How did you meet him?"

The face of the man on the table contorted in a mental fight to avoid answering, but to no avail. "I've known Chen . . . for a long time . . . back when he was working the streets."

"You had just finished school?"

"Yes . . . I was a user . . . Chen's people supplied me."

"How long have you been working with him against Hue Yen?"

"Not long," the voice said in a flat whisper. "I've only been . . . close to the great Hue Yen . . . for three years. Chen approached me again . . . at this time."

"I thought he was secluded."

"He had me taken . . . to a place . . . where we could

communicate by video. He's become . . . so fat he can't move out . . . of his house," the small Chinese said, his answers coming slowly, his will still trying to fight but without success.

"I've seen the evidence in your house, Quang. You planned to cross both sides, the Russians *and* Chen. You planned to take over from Hue Yen yourself. How? Where was your strength?"

"I have support . . . in Kuala Lumpur. People . . . you don't know about. People Chen . . . doesn't know about."

"But you can't be sure of that. Did you know that Chen had most of his people carrying transmitters? They were implanted under the skin."

"My God," the voice said languidly. The expression seemed strange without the usual emphasis.

"He probably had your people infiltrated. Some probably had transmitter implants. He probably knows every move you made and every plan you were cooking up against him."

"It's not . . . possible."

"More than possible. Very probable. So the Russians have been destroyed, but Chen's going to use you. You can't defeat him. You're not the man he is. You know that."

"He's an . . . an evil man."

"Explain. Tell me something I don't know."

"The House. A place called the House. He uses it to tear . . . to tear people down. Interrogates them. Forces them to his will."

"It's been destroyed. All the guards and prisoners have been killed. Tell me something I don't know."

"All prisoners who survived . . . House . . . working as

slaves. Those who died . . . buried in special place that grows . . . every day."

He listened while Quang told him of the slave factories throughout Malaysia run by Chen. While he had a photographic memory, he didn't try to retain it all. He'd make sure Samantha gave the tape to Chief Windsor. That was his department.

"So Chen is a mass murderer."

"Life to . . . to Chen . . . is a quantity . . . that can be . . . bought and sold . . . and terminated at . . . at his will."

"Where is Chen?" Carter asked, throwing the question in unexpectedly.

"In his house."

"Which house? He had more than one."

"His house. Lives in the one on Telok Blangah Road near Ginseng Essense Balm Park," Quang said, his voice more distinct, less slurred, as if he'd subconsciously come to a decision and was no longer afraid.

"You're sure of this?"

"Yes."

"The plans I took from your house are for this same house?"

"They're all indentical."

"Anyone else in the house with him?"

"Just an old retainer. Been with Chen for many years. Someone has to feed the fat slob, to bathe him, and move him around."

Carter sat for a moment thinking about what he'd learned. Quang went through a spasm. His face contorted.

"Have you ever had heart problems?" Carter asked, an urgency in his voice.

"Small attack five years ago. Hue Yen doesn't know. No one knows."

And they probably never will, Carter thought as the man writhed on the table, his face contorted. Carter turned off the tape recorder and watched for a moment while the writhing stopped and the face became serene in death. The odds were against the small man from the start. He'd played in a game he was ill prepared for and paid the supreme penalty. Another problem to hand over to Chief Windsor.

He untied Quang and wrapped his body in black plastic he found in the shipping room. He lit a cigarette and waited for Samantha to return. It was seven-thirty.

It was almost over. Or it was close to being over. Chen was the monster he'd suspected all along. The man placed no value on human life, and that had nothing to do with size or appearance.

He felt a kind of catharsis. It happened to him before. You are sent out to terminate a man, to solve a problem, and no matter how many times you have done it before, it eats at your guts. Unless. Unless you find that your target is truly a man without regard for life. A man who will kill untold hundreds if you don't stop him.

He dragged on the cigarette and thought about how he was going to do it.

TWELVE

"You really threw me a curve with those shields, but they'll be ready by noon," Samantha said as she returned, somewhat out of breath. "Hey! Where's Quang?"

Carter pointed to the roll of black plastic. "Sometimes the drug is too strong. He had a heart condition I didn't know about."

She looked at him with dulled eyes for a moment as if she was totally unaccustomed to death.

"I don't enjoy this," he told her, as if reading her thoughts. "He was a stupid man but he was also an evil one."

"What did you find out?"

"Chen is much worse than we expected," he said as he punched the eject button on the tape deck. "Chief Windsor will have to dispose of Quang for us. And we'll give him the tape. It seems that Chen has slave shops all over Ma-

149

laysia. Quang also told me about a private burial ground where Chen has planted a lot of evidence."

"What do you mean?"

"Anyone who was processed through the House and lived was sent to the slave markets. Those who died were buried," Carter said flatly.

She shuddered at the thought. "So what's next?" she asked.

"I want to take Chen or destroy him before dark. We've got a lot to do."

"What's first?"

"Call Chief Windsor. Ask him to come over. Tell him it's urgent."

"Let me get this straight," Chief Windsor said, taking a gulp from the beer Carter had poured for him. "You want me to turn my back no matter what reports I get later in the day?"

"We'll call you just before going in."

"We? Surely you're not involving Samantha in this."

"It's her territory. She's a professional. She wants to be in on it."

They both looked at Samantha. She nodded. "There's no way you can keep me out."

Chief Windsor shook his head, his expression grim, "The tape," he said, changing the subject. "What did you say is on it?"

"Quang told me a lot about Chen's operation. The worst part is kidnappings by the hundreds, orientation, and ultimately slave labor in hundreds of factories around Malaysia. That was the function of the House. It was the starting point on a chain of horror for thousands."

"The worst part to me is the private burial grounds he has for all those who don't make it. It could add up to thousands," Samantha added.

"And this is the man who was going to control Quang when Hue Yen gave up office," the police chief said, swigging the last of his beer.

"Gave up office?" Carter said. "Why would a man like Chen wait that long?"

Chief Windsor sat for a long minute digesting the thought. "He wouldn't, of course. It's all so damned diabolical. A great man like Hue Yen. He has no idea. It's going to hit him hard."

"It's your job to tell him when we've finished our job," Carter said. "Play him the tape. Tell him about the House and the Russians."

"What about the Soo brothers?" Samantha asked.

"I think Chief Windsor will find their bones in Chen's graveyard," Carter said. "My job was to find the Soo brothers and make sure Hue Yen's position was secured. When Chen is dead, it will be over."

"You can't bring him in? Be much better," Chief Windsor said.

"No chance as I see it. I've studied the plans for Chen's fortress. We'll have to blast our way in and end it for him any way we can," Carter explained. "It's the best way, you know," he went on, sipping the last of his beer. "If we were able to turn him over to you, your troubles would just be beginning."

"A bloody war," Chief Windsor muttered shaking his head.

"And you keep clear no matter the pressure. It shouldn't take more than a half hour if my plan works," Carter explained. "But it will sound like all hell has broken loose when it does go down."

When Chief Windsor had left, a sadder but wiser man, Samantha was eager to get the show on the road.

"We have to check Quang's information on the Chen mansion," Carter told her. "I don't want to go in without being sure."

"And how do we do that?"

"Stakeout. I figure if we watch all three houses for an hour each we can make a fairly good judgment."

"Which one first?"

"The obvious. The one Quang fingered on Telok Blangah road. If we don't see any sign of life at all, we try the one on Pioneer Road, then the one on Lady Hill Road."

"I've got an old Chevy with black glass windows I've used for stakeouts. We'll take it," she offered.

"Sounds good. When we're sure, we come back here one last time and I'll go over the plan with you."

They sat in the Chevy on Ayer Rajah Road, each with strong field glasses, looking down at the mansion one block south on Telok Blangah Road. Carter was still in the black outfit. Samantha had dressed similarly and had put black greasepaint on her beautiful face. The car smelled of the beer and sandwiches she'd brought. It was hot through noon and on to one o'clock. The car was like an oven.

"How's the wrist?" Carter asked during the boring wait.

"Not bad. It throbs a lot. I suspect it's getting more action than the doctor prescribed."

"We'll be finished and back at the safe house in a couple of hours. You can get all the attention you want then."

"That a promise?" She leered at him through the makeup.

Carter's smile opened some of the cracks in his lips and gashes in his cheeks he'd brought back from the beating. Samantha had treated his face as best she could, and had applied a base coat of oil before putting on his camouflage makeup. His face ached and called out for attention, but he tried to ignore it. In the action to come, he knew it would not be a handicap and that was all that mattered.

They sat. Nothing significant had happened until Carter asked, "You see what I see?"

"Bingo!"

"Right. Looks like a provisions truck."

They watched while the driver pressed a buzzer set in the stone wall surrounding the main gate. After a conversation with someone, he was admitted. He drove to the back of the house and a small Oriental man came out to help him unload.

"There's enough there for a small hotel," Samantha said. Her face was wreathed in smiles.

"Or one very fat man," Carter added. He, too, was delighted with some final proof.

"So we're on to the next phase," she said.

"Back to the safe house," he ordered.

She drove with care through the midday downtown traffic to the rooms behind the store. It was close to two when she parked and they went in.

The place had been cleaned up. The body was gone. Samantha's people had cleared away the empty beer bottles and emptied the ashtrays.

Samantha brewed a pot of coffee and sat across the table from Carter. "What now?" she asked.

"Where are the shields?" he asked.

She produced two shields made of an oval mirror with a layer of Lexan attached. Holes had been drilled through the glass and Lexan, probably with diamond drills, and insulated handles were bolted on the inside. Carter hefted one. They were not too heavy, at least not for him.

"Try one," he suggested. "How does it feel?"

"Heavy. How long will I have to hold it?"

"Ten minutes if we're lucky. A half hour if we're not."

"I can handle that. What are they for?"

"The robots are equipped with both laser beams and 40mm machine guns," Carter explained. "The Lexan will deflect the bullets; the mirrors will take care of the lasers."

"We'll have to make sure we're not too close. We could deflect the rays at each other."

"We have to work close together, so we'll have to be very careful," he explained.

"We could work close together now." She smiled lasciviously. "Isn't that the line that soldiers use when going into battle?"

He pecked on the lips. "There's nothing I'd like better, Sam. But business first."

"Right," she sighed. "How are we going to strike back?"

He moved to the closet where she'd secreted the cesta and Howard Schmidt's case. He opened the case and took out one of the grenades. "One of Howard's latest goodies," he said.

"He's always trying to get me to use things like those. Not my style," she explained.

"I feel the same, but you have to adapt. How would you tackle the robots?"

She thought for a moment.

"How many robots? Six or seven along the perimeter? Another half-dozen roaming the grounds?"

"Half and half. An even dozen," he replied.

"Impossible."

"I don't think so," he said, examining the cesta. "Do you have a coat hanger and wire cutters?"

"Doesn't every self-respecting spy?" she asked, dryly, getting up and going to a closet.

Carter quickly fashioned a hook out of the coat hanger. It was small, about three inches long. He secured it to the inside of the cesta near the wrist bands and left one end to act as a hook. Then he strapped on the cesta.

She watched, still puzzled, until he took one of the grenades and carefully hung its release pin on the hook.

"You know how to use that thing?" she asked.

"I've had some lessons from an expert."

"Tell me about it."

"It's long story. Take my word for it." He looked at his borrowed watch: it was just past three. He had four hours until dark and he wanted it ended by dark. "Do you know a very private place on this island?" he asked.

"Sure. Why?"

"We're going to do some training. It couldn't hurt."

She carried the case and he took the cesta. "Do you have any submachine guns around here?" he asked.

"You want submachine guns too? Why?"

"Not for the house. For general use."

"In the Chevy. There are two Uzi machine pistols in the trunk."

"Put them up front. They can't do us any good sitting in the trunk."

She drove while he kept a lookout for unwanted company. She picked a spot in the Yishun area not far from the causeway. While she drove, he fashioned a few crude grenades from material he'd brought along.

She pulled into dense brush and led him to an open area that she'd obviously used for target practice.

"Perfect," Carter said, strapping on the cesta and making sure the hook was secure.

He swung the basket around a few times, getting back the feel of it. He thought of Eloise but forced her from his mind. This wasn't the time or place.

He picked up a few rocks the size of the grenades and used the cesta to toss them at the remains of shattered bottles on a riddled log. His aim was true. Not a shard of glass remained on the log.

"I'm impressed," Samantha said, watching the rocks speed to their targets with unerring accuracy.

"That's the easy part," he said, handing her the substitute grenades he'd made on the way there.

"What do I do?" she asked.

"Picture the house while standing at the front gate," he said. "A double steel fence starts next to the stonework of the gate. The two fences are about twelve feet apart, chain link, electrified, almost impossible to cut."

"And the robots circling inside."

"Right. I'm going to be to your left with the cesta on my right arm. You hook on the grenades and I toss them. I'll tell you the time settings for each. We should be able to toss one every five to ten seconds."

"Sounds simple enough."

"The robot will be firing at us. So you have to hold your shield on your right arm and feed the grenades with your left."

"Figures. Nothin's ever easy."

"The forty-millimeter slugs will feel like ninety-mile-an-hour baseballs hitting your shield."

"They'll knock me over," Samantha protested.

"You'll have to do your best. We have to protect ourselves as well as we can. Even then, if the robots have artificial intelligence or Chen can control them individually, they could aim at our feet and we'll be in big trouble."

"Shit, Carter, you're crazy. This isn't going to work," she grumbled dejectedly.

"It'll work if we can fight smoothly as a team. We'll beat them to the punch," he said. "These little babies Howard gave us are so powerful they'll probably toss a robot ten to twenty feet into the air. Their electronic circuits will be destroyed immediately."

She looked at him skeptically, then assumed her position. She held her shield in her right hand and he took his in his left. She attached a phony grenade and he slung it. They pitched a dozen or more until she was beginning to feel confident.

"Now we try it from our knees," he said.

She looked at him as if he were insane but knew he was right. If they attacked standing all the way, it would be a miracle if they weren't cut down at the legs.

"We kneel and fire off a few. Then we assume another attack zone and kneel again. Come on. We'll try one with a live grenade, move to a new location, and try another."

"Okay. But I still think you're nuts."

"That tree stump fifty feet to your left is a robot bearing down on us and firing. You hook on a live grenade and we move quickly twenty feet to the left. You hook on another grenade and I destroy that oak tree fifty feet to my left.

"You ready?"

"Why not? We might as well give it a shot."

"Set them both at five seconds. Ready? On the count of three. One. Two. Three!"

She hooked on the grenade and he tossed. They moved twenty feet to their left and she hooked on again. Partway to their new position the ground shook, almost throwing them off their feet. But she hooked on again and he tossed at the tree.

They clung to the ground, their shields in place in front of them until all was still.

Samantha poked her head out. "Holy Mother of God!" she breathed. Only a crater remained where the huge stump had stood. The oak tree, two feet in diameter at the base, was shattered, only a foot of ragged stump remaining in the ground.

"What do you think?" Carter asked, brushing the dirt and debris from his head.

"I think we need hard hats and something to cover our ears. Hot damn! We can blow him off the map with these."

"With the robots firing at us, don't forget."

"I won't forget," she said, climbing into the Chevy, a huge grin spread over her face. "I never knew how much fun little-boy war games were," she joked.

"It's not fun in real life," he said as they pulled away. "I've seen too many battlefields. Bodies scattered everywhere—blood and guts covered with clouds of flies—the stink enough to drive you insane."

"Hey. Don't scare me," she said in a softer voice.

"Just don't get too cocky. If we act as a team, like we did just now, we'll cream Chen's robots. If not, kiss the world good-bye."

He felt the adrenaline pumping and knew she felt the same way. He was so wrapped up in his thoughts that he didn't see the car following until the glass of the Chevy's rear window was shattered by small-arms fire.

"Head back for the brush!" he shouted over the noise.

He grabbed for an Uzi, opened a window, and leaned out. The other car had gained on them but was swerving from left to right. He emptied a clip without hitting anything vital. He reached into Howard's case and took out one of the precious grenades. It was set for ten seconds. He leaned out the window, waited for exactly the right moment with bullets flying all around him, and pulled the pin.

He tossed the small ball to bounce once and land under the pursuing car. The roar that followed was deafening. They crashed through the brush for another fifty feet, then circled back to the crater where the car had been, their radiator blowing steam from a tree trunk that had punctured it.

All that was left of their attackers was a twisted hunk of metal burning furiously. They couldn't find a body, but Samantha found out what he'd meant about a battleground. Flies swarmed in by the thousands. Small pieces of flesh and bone could be found over a fifty-foot area. She stared, her mouth open, one tear coursing down her cheek.

"The battle's begun," he said.

THIRTEEN

The Chevy left behind at the site of the afternoon skirmish, Samantha Trail drove a GMC Jimmy along Keppel Road and turned off at the Ayer Rajah Expressway. She was scared. In all the years she'd worked for Hawk, nothing she'd done had approached this. For the first time she was aware of her mortality, and the thought sent a chill up her spine.

Carter sat calmly beside her. He had the cesta across his lap and was smoking a cigarette. She wondered if he, too, was frightened. Maybe not. He'd been through this kind of thing many times, she was sure. No wonder the whole intelligence community looked on him as their top gun.

Chen sat in his chair, a huge platter of steaming food in front of him. His hands were at his sides, the chopsticks still on the table. For once in his life, his mind wasn't on food when it was there for the taking.

They had told him that Quang was dead. Quang, the simple fool who had defied him, was dead. He didn't mourn for the stupid man, but he mourned the loss of opportunity. It had taken him more than three years to insinuate Quang into the position of power he'd occupied.

He could have had it all. Singapore first, then the Malay Peninsula and Penang, then Sumatra and the rest of Malaysia. All of it was lost to him. And all because of one man.

Who was this gnat that buzzed around him, taking a bite here, a nibble there? The man was the most persistent antagonist Chen had ever had. And now the nibbles had become huge chunks. The loss of Quang had been critical.

He'd had this man Carter in his power twice and lost him. How could that happen? How could the man be taken by the Russians and come away unscathed and all the Russians dead? He wasn't a superman. He was flesh and blood. He's seen his men beat the man's face almost to a pulp and still he'd escaped. He'd escaped to carry on and finally kill Quang.

Something else haunted him. What had Quang told the man Carter before he died? The American devil man probably knew about the headquarters house. He even had an architect's plan of the house's layout.

Fear grabbed at him for the first time in years and he shook it off. Carter could not get to him. He had too many layers of defense, some that only he knew about. The men who had built them for him were in a common grave, silent and cold.

As he thought of the foolproof defenses, some hidden and very secret, his confidence returned and he began to eat. Let the foolish Carter come. Even if he knew about the layout of the house, even if he knew of the robots and the fences, even if he knew about all of these things and could somehow destroy them, he couldn't know about the secondary defenses and the third. He would never break through, not all the way.

The thought of the intruder's death brought him pleasure and he ate with gusto. He knew how to manipulate the robots, how to override the automatic sequences programmed into them and control them with the series of joy sticks built into his massive console. He'd spent countless hours manipulating the robots and, like the teen-agers of the city in the video game arcades, he could defeat anyone who stood against him.

The system had only one weakness. If he took over the robots and fought his battle using his own wits, he also overrode the protection programs that guaranteed the robots would never fire on each other. No matter. In all the hours of practice, he had never come close to firing on his own robots.

Death was an aphrodisiac for the fat man. Sex had been impossible for him for years, but the death of a stubborn enemy or a beautiful woman gave him gratification, almost a sexual thrill. Carter's death would be the ultimate joy.

Carter, the Killmaster, ready to go into action, sat unmoving, his cigarette long since crushed in the Jimmy's ashtray, his mind tuned to the teachings of his yoga guru of long ago. His thoughts were not fogged by emotion or fear. They were tuned to the tools he brought into battle: the superbly conditioned body; the experience that could be matched by no other man alive; the weapons he'd devised for this particular encounter. Back at the safe house he'd gone over the impending battle in his mind a score of times and found a glaring weakness in his defenses. Always conscious of having the best defense possible, at the last moment he'd asked Samantha to have her craftsmen prepare a large sheet of Lexan backed up by a mirror. Now it was secured to the top of the Jimmy on a carrying rack, a sheet similar to their shields but measuring six feet by ten.

"Drive to within a hundred feet of the main gate and park the vehicle parallel to the fence," he ordered calmly.

Samantha seemed to pull herself out of a trance and followed his orders. As soon as the vehicle had stopped, he jumped out and used Hugo to slash the bindings holding the large sheet of Lexan. It was heavy and awkward to handle. Samantha came around to his side and helped him ease it down so that it leaned against the Jimmy on the far side facing the fence.

The two agents, now fully prepared, worked behind their barrier. Carter slipped on the cesta and tied it as he'd been taught. He checked the small hook and found that it was secure.

Samantha opened Schmidt's case and filled the pockets of a carpenter's apron she'd borrowed from one of her people. It held all the high-explosive grenades in the large pocket on the left side, and the phosphorous ones in the smaller pocket on the right.

Carter picked up one of the shields. He held it with his left hand and stood on Samantha's left.

Samantha held her shield in her right hand and palmed a grenade in her left.

They moved away from the protection of the Jimmy, staying close together.

"Set the first one for fifteen seconds. I'll lay it at the base of the fence."

Samantha's hand shook as she set the dial. It was difficult to do with one hand, but she'd practiced incessantly and managed it in a second or two. "Loaded," she said. It was the signal they had agreed on earlier.

Carter was in no hurry. They were out in the open now. Their purpose had to be obvious, but there was no special action from the robots who continued to patrol the entire perimeter as usual. Perhaps they weren't programmed to react to people outside the fence unless attacked.

But what about Chen? Carter wondered. Surely he knew they were out there. Then the answer hit him. Chen could only be an observer for the moment. He was at the mercy of the software that controlled his electronic guards. Whether or not he had manual override, they'd probably learn later.

What would he do if he were Chen? The answer was simple. He'd do nothing. Not for the present. Nothing had really happened except a threat and it could be a bluff.

It was time to show him they weren't bluffing. He swung the cesta around in a perfect arc, the timing just right, and let the grenade drop at the bottom of the outer fence about ten feet to the left of the rock wall.

They both knelt and waited for the concussion, remembering the practice session in the woods.

The explosion was deafening and was followed by the crackle of severed high-tension wires. Debris and earth showered down on them from above. Samantha shook her head, a habit she'd always had to dislodge foreign objects from her hair, forgetting that she was not only bald, but protected by a steel helmet. She grinned sheepishly and hooked on a grenade set for ten seconds as previously agreed.

"Loaded," she said.

•   •   •

The explosion shook the house slightly. Chen jumped and cried out as if the grenade had gone off beside him. The steel chair bearing his weight groaned but held him. He had been watching Carter and the woman on his monitors. Their preparations had been comic and he'd enjoyed a chuckle as he saw them place what looked like a giant mirror in place.

Now nothing was amusing. When the smoke cleared, a gaping hole had been torn in the fence at least a dozen feet across and the lasers in the area were out of commission. The robots had reacted as programmed and were wheeling toward the intrusion from both directions. The big man decided to let them handle it for the present. They had never been tested under actual conditions, but had met every possible threat thrown at them in hundreds of simulations.

In the kitchen above the control room, Chen's man screamed as the roar shook the house. A pot of boiling eels toppled from the stove and spilled over his sandaled feet. He hopped around in pain not knowing what was happening. Despite his scalded feet, he ran down the long narrow flight of stairs to his pantry two floors below. If the attack he'd expected ever since coming to work for the fat man was about to start, he wanted to be close to an exit.

Carter poked his head around one side of the huge shield and saw the robots coming toward the opening at high speed. When the first one reached the hole in the fence, the Killmaster moved out into the open and let fly with a grenade. It landed under the nearest robot and lay in the dirt for all of five seconds before going off.

The robot flew into the air and a massive shock wave hit

the two out in the open. They scrambled to their knees and held the shields in front of them.

Three robots drawn to the scene obeyed preprogrammed orders and opened fire with lasers and automatic weapons. The laser beams were reflected off their shields at odd angles, but the 40mm slugs rained against the Lexan, almost knocking Samantha over.

The woman recovered, set a grenade to fire at seven seconds, and shouted, "Loaded. Seven seconds."

Two of the robots were at the opening and a third was close by. Carter aimed the third grenade between the two electronic guards, then ducked as another shock wave hit them.

"Get behind the Jimmy!" he shouted at Samantha.

They moved from their knees and stayed low as they eased to the right and back behind the wall of Lexan, small-arms fire bouncing off their shields, almost knocking Samantha over again.

Carter peeked around the side of the Jimmy on one side and Samantha followed his lead at the other. The two robots they had attacked lay on their sides, partly destroyed, aflame, their lasers aimed harmlessly at the evening sky.

"Did we get them?" Samantha shouted over her shoulder.

"I think so. The first was a perfect hit. The other two are damaged and will probably poop out altogether as their circuits cook."

"So that's three down and nine to do," she said.

"As far as we know. Set the next one for fifteen seconds. I want to try something."

Carter heard her call out that she was ready as he eased to his left again. This time two robots were waiting for them and let fly with everything they had as soon as the two humans were in the open. Steel-jacketed 40mm projectiles rained against their shields as they moved to the left on their knees.

The Killmaster swung the cesta in a graceful arc, using more loft. The small round explosive was in the air for three seconds and landed beneath a robot that was standing off about fifty yards waiting to attack.

The explosion destroyed the robot, but the shock wave didn't disturb Carter and Samantha as much as the others had. While they crept back to the safety of their mirrored barrier, Carter found he could direct the reflection of lasers from his shield at specific targets. Before they were back behind the Jimmy, his deflections had destroyed the two damaged robots. Four down for sure and only two left between the perimeter fences.

The sound of the first four grenades could be heard all across the city. The disciplined citizens of Singapore were conditioned to law and order. They huddled in small groups wondering why they had not heard police sirens. The noise had been going on for three or four minutes. It sounded as if they city were under attack. Where were the police who were normally very visible?

The man who knew what was going on sat in his office, a look of anguish on his face. Twice in the past minute or two, his aides had interrupted to implore him to take some action and twice he had shouted at them to follow orders. No official action was to be taken.

The phone rang. He picked it up. "The prime minister is on line two," a disembodied voice told him.

He reached out wearily to push a button. "Windsor," was all he said.

"Hue Yen. What is happening, Chalkie?"

The prime minister was a man who always came right to the point.

"You'd find any explanation difficult to believe, Mr. Prime Minister," Chief Windsor said.

"Try me."

"I'd prefer to let it run its course and cover the whole story with you when it's over."

"When what is over?"

"I'd prefer not to say."

"Are your men involved?"

"No."

"No? Then who?"

"I'd prefer not to say right now."

"You will tell me right now or I will order out the army," Hue Yen said, his voice rising for the first time.

"Sir, believe me, it's best to leave it alone for a few more minutes."

"Tell me what you know, Windsor, or I swear—"

"It will be finished before you can muster the troops, Mr. Prime Minister. Believe me."

"I've trusted you through the years. You know that. You know the opposition I've had to keep you . . ."

"I know and I appreciate it, sir. Just go with me one more time," Chief Windsor pleaded. "This is very important, life or death for your government, perhaps for all of Southeast Asia. Please, sir, leave it with me. Give me another half hour."

"All right. But my phone is ringing off the hook. You'd better be right, Chalkie. And you'd better have one hell of a story for me."

Chief Windsor sat at his desk for what seemed like long minutes, agonizing over the situation. Then he poured himself another scotch but dropped it on the floor when another explosion rocked the city.

All the remaining robots were concentrated not far from the hole in the fence now. They had been programmed to stay far enough apart to avoid grenade attacks and multiple losses. Carter started to ease out for the next attack. He had learned something from his earlier forays and was determined to try out a theory this time.

He'd heard Samantha's cry of "Loaded!" as soon as they'd reached the saftey of the shield. With a live grenade in the cesta and his shield in his other hand, he was ready for the worst.

And the worst was what he got. The two remaining first-line robots were close to the hole in the fence and the other half dozen were ranged inside the second fence, all firing at him as he moved out. He felt a steel projectile crease his shoe as he launched another grenade at the closest robot.

This time he didn't move back to safety. Samantha pulled at his cesta arm before she realized he intended to stay out. She remained beside him, her shield in place, waiting.

Three robots fired from the right, inside the grounds, and three from the left. The fifth robot in the fence perimeter was a smoldering ruin. The last of the front-line robots was concentrating on Samantha.

Carter deftly maneuvered his shield with his left hand until he had a feel for how the laser beams reflected from the mirrored surface. The streams were almost constant. He watched the deflected beams move to the left until they were directed at the group of three inside the fence, far to the left. Just before he motioned Samantha to duck back inside the barrier, he saw the beams converge on one of the distant robots but he didn't see if the maneuver had helped.

Samantha let out a triumphant whoop. "You got one of the bastards!" she shouted.

"Reflected lasers?" he asked.

"It was beautiful! Blew the damned thing to bits!" she said delighted.

"Six down. That's half. And we've got most of our grenades left," he said, almost as excited as she.

"The rest of it's going to be harder, isn't it?" she asked.

"I'm afraid so. We can't retreat behind the big shield much longer."

"Can't we move it closer? Maybe if we propped it up between two wrecked robots?"

"Good thought. But it's too heavy. We'd be vulnerable, couldn't hold out small shields. There's no way it could be done."

"What do we do now?"

"One more sortie to get the last of the outer group. One more to blow the inner fence. Then we'll have to play it by ear," he said. "Make the next one seven seconds."

"You're wounded!" she said, spotting the crease across his boot that had nicked his toes and produced blood. It looked a lot worse than it was.

He looked her over. She had two laser burns: one on her right arm, the other on her left ankle. "Not a problem. What about the burns? How do they feel?" he asked.

"I can't feel them yet. Maybe later. Let's get this over with."

He moved out and let fly the grenade she'd set for seven seconds. Without waiting for instructions, she set another for seven seconds and shouted its readiness over the first explosion.

Carter tossed another grenade through the opening in the fence. It landed at the base of the second fence and exploded immediately.

The concussion of two closely spaced explosions knocked them both over. For a moment they were both vulnerable, flat on their backs, their shields held skyward.

Carter couldn't help Samantha. He had both hands full. She had her left hand free. She'd have to make it on her own.

Samantha had never experienced anything like this in her life and never wanted to again.

Her arm hurt and so did her ankle. She had lied about the laser burns. They hurt so much it was all she could do to keep from screaming.

The second fence had been breached and seven robots had been destroyed. She'd been skeptical that it could be done, but now she knew better. She knew now that they could defeat Chen, then he wasn't invulnerable, but she also knew that the worst part was yet to come.

The specter of death was back with her. The last time it had been merely a feeling of danger, a concern for her mortality. But this time she felt a cold chill run down her spine as the hooded man with the scythe was standing in the field of battle and he was looking directly at her.

The fat man couldn't believe what was happening to his defenses. Seven of the robots were destroyed. The inner barrier had been breached. He was a shaking mass of blubber, his hands almost out of his control as he switched over to manual override and brought the five remaining robots to the hole in the inner fence, positioned in a semicircle, their awesome weapons pointed at the gaping hole.

The two in black couldn't stay behind the big shield forever. They had to come out and fight if they expected to enter the second barrier. He held on to the joy sticks of the two leading robots, his hands a little more steady, and watched the video screen with bloodshot eyes.

The grounds outside the mansion smelled of cordite and electronic fires. Carter thought he could smell burning flesh but he wrote it off as imagination. The worst was yet to come. They had to move out into the open and stay there, fighting every inch of the way. He turned to his partner.

"It's going to be twice as bad from here on in. I'm not sure I want to expose you to it."

"You don't have a choice. Load!" she called out. "Ten seconds!"

He moved out. The rays and bullets of five robots met him in an almost overwhelming assault. He stole a glance at Samantha. She was undergoing the same wicked barrage.

Something unusual was happening. In a semicircle, a battle formation that had never been programmed for them, the robots were coming under as much fire as their targets. Five sets of lasers aimed at the two shields were being beamed directly back at them. Before the monster inside could react and go back on automatic defense, three of the robots had been melted down and the other two, programmed to regain automatic sequencing, were turning to take up new positions.

Carter heard a war whoop beside him as he let fly with another grenade. He could see the last two robots as they maneuvered into new defensive positions. The small round ball dropped with deadly accuracy under the wheels of one and blew it twenty feet into the air, spinning, a twisted piece of metal filled with smoking wires.

He motioned Samantha to move forward through the gas as she hooked on another grenade and called out, "Loaded! Ten seconds!"

They moved in on the last robot. Carter knew they'd been lucky so far. Every one of the robots had been a deadly killing machine and they still had one to go. Whoever had programmed them had allowed for any possible scenario, even this one. The robot was cagey. It didn't show itself but stayed behind one of the wrecks and fired constantly.

This would be one of the toughest shots he'd ever made. Unlike tennis, the lob shot in jai alai wasn't common. He thought about the shot until it was firm in his mind, then let his brain direct his arm and the cesta in a higher arc that sent the small ball in the highest pitch he'd ever tried.

Everything from that point on seemed to be in slow motion. The ball flew away to move slowly through the air. The 40mm slugs still rained on their shields. The robot, hull down but with enough clearance to allow for full firepower, was etched against the fading light to their right.

The grenade exploded. It had landed five feet in front of the robot, not a perfect hit but enough to toss the ingenious machine backward a dozen feet and neutralize its electronic circuits.

The battlefield was quiet for a few minutes, then the silence was broken by Samantha's happy laughter as she dropped her shield and danced around Carter in a victory celebration that was born out of pure joy and relief. It was a release from mortal fear. It was an escape from the Grim Reaper. It was the beginning of the new life she had dreamed of.

Smoke rose from the broken hulks. Craters had changed the carefully tended grounds to a moonscape. The smell was of electronic, not human death. At last Carter permitted himself a smile as he watched Samantha dance with joy.

He put down his shield and unstrapped the cesta, and couldn't help but laugh with her.

While he grinned at her and held out his arms, a beam of red light flashed from a dead robot, a freak discharge from a loaded condenser. It caught Samantha in one eye and exited out the back of her skull, sending her helmet flying and frying her brain in the passing.

Carter stood, frozen, then he ran to her as she crumpled to the ground. He held her for a moment, looking at the smoke drift from inside her skull, feeling for a pulse but knowing none would be there.

Something snapped inside the usually disciplined brain. He untied the apron from her waist and tied it around his own, all the while raining curses on the head of the man who lived in the big stone house.

With rage taking the place of reason, and with a searing hatred coursing through his body, he tossed one of the remaining high-explosive grenades at the building, knocking huge chunks of rock from the solid wall but not penetrating the citadel of Fat Chen.

Then he fell to his knees and rocked back and forth, holding Samantha's body as if it were a child he were crooning to sleep.

FOURTEEN

As Carter sat amid the debris, maniacal laughter boomed out from the house. Chen was celebrating his victory, and the sound of his voice filled the man from AXE with loathing. Men like Chen were uncommon. The man on the street almost never encountered them, never read about them in the papers, but Carter knew of them. He had met too many and the experience was beginning to weary him, drain him of his usual steel resolve to rid the world of them. You couldn't make demands on your mind and body as Carter had for so long without some burnout.

The voice boomed on, laughing, cursing, using English, Mandarin, Cantonese, and a half-dozen other languages. The sound attacked Carter like a bombardment from the robots. He raised his head from the lifeless body he held and looked at the mansion. Chen stood behind a huge plate glass window, his huge bulk filling the space, his caver-

177

nous mouth open, his voice still booming out his victory speech, his eyes laughing at the man kneeling on the ground.

Carter stared at Fat Chen. So this was the monster who was responsible for it all. At last they were face to face. The expression on the Killmaster's face slowly changed from sadness to hatred and finally to resolve. The spirit of revenge grew to fill him almost to bursting as he looked at the man who had sent thousands to die and three times that number to live in slavery.

Carter stood up shakily. He was cut and bleeding in a score of places from the shrapnel his own mad attack had produced. He should have felt weak, a candidate for a hospital bed, but he seemed to be infused with an inner strength that was built on a glowing ember of hatred he could never extinguish until Chen was dead.

With the efficiency of long practice, the Killmaster's right hand slipped his Luger from its holster and, in a single fluid motion, put three shots in a close triangular pattern at the monster's massive forehead.

The laughter continued. The window was bulletproof, just as Carter's shield had been. For a moment, the anger and frustration he'd experienced at Samantha's death returned, and he emptied Wilhelmina at the man behind the transparent wall.

While he looked at his gargantuan enemy, the hidden speakers that sent out the man's voice boomed out a message:

"Good-bye, Carter. I'm going to throw out one more challenge for you and I'll be gone. Do you hear me, Carter? I won't be here when you finally figure out how to get to me."

A cold determination had taken the place of rage. The

Killmaster had come close to irrational action but that had passed. Carter looked up at the enemy who still stood behind his barrier, then watched as Chen moved toward the massive wooden door at the front of the house.

"One more deterrent, Carter," the monster's voice boomed out.

Carter saw him reach for a lever beside him and pull it. In an almost deafening clatter of sound, steel bars fell from concealed envelopes to cover every door and window. The whole house was cocooned in steel and stone, the walls three feet thick, the bars too strong for his weapons, the windows undoubtedly all of Lexan.

Chen's man sat on a stool in the pantry next to the kitchen and held his hands over his ears. He had almost gone insane while the bombardment was going on outside. He'd thought the house was going to tumble around him as the madman outside tossed explosives at the house. Thank God their attacker had not aimed one at a door, or by this time he would be inside.

Now the voice of his master was driving him mad. It was all too much. And it wasn't fair. He was the only one who would look after the fat pig. He'd been promised riches beyond his wildest dreams if he would stay. He'd also been threatened with a life of slavery if he left.

The bars slid into place with a loud metallic clanging.

Curse all the gods! He was trapped! He had to get out somehow. What was the madman outside doing? He couldn't see a thing for the dirt on the pantry windows. He'd been meaning to clean them, but he had too many other things to do.

●   ●   ●

Chen left the huge window and waddled on swollen feet to a steel chair in a room he sometimes used for sleeping. It was time to get out. A portion of the floor in the next room would lower him to the basement and the escape tunnel that led to another house and ultimate safety. He had an armored car waiting that would take his weight. A loyal employee was on hand every hour of the day and night to drive for him.

A loud chuckle bubbled up in his throat as he thought of the futile efforts of the man outside. He might have been outraged at the loss of his robots, but he could operate from another headquarters. He'd made arrangements for the future. He'd set up decoy mansions that were identical to this one. But his real ace in the hole was a stronghold he'd built on Penang, off the coast of Malaysia, the paradise island in the Strait of Malacca.

But what was the hurry? He'd not be able to eat in transit. He pulled the cord for his man and waited, but nothing happened. That damned Heu Choy was probably petrified with fear. No matter. He pushed a button and a large tray swiveled out of a concealed closet. It was filled with cold meats, chilled seafood, raw vegetables, pickles, and fresh and preserved fruits.

Let the damned American drive himself mad trying to find a chink in my armor. While the thought occurred, a missile of some kind bounced off the window and exploded in a burst of flame outside.

The monster that was Arthur Cecil Chen roared with laughter, bits of half-chewed food falling from his mouth.

Carter had circled the mansion, carefully, like a predatory jungle cat in the night. He was unable to find one place in the mansion that looked more vulnerable than another. In frustration, he pulled the pin on one of the half-dozen phosphorous grenades he carried and flung it as hard as he could at a lighted second-floor window. It bounced off and exploded not far from him.

Fingers of fire reached out in every direction. Pieces of phosphorous burning at more than a thousand degrees Fahrenheit started fires in a score of places. Two small fragments caught in his clothing and he had to roll over and over in the deep grass to extinguish them. Where they had been, three-inch holes still smoldered in Carter's clothes and his skin was badly blistered.

In the pantry, Heu Choy, Chen's man, stood on the stool and frantically pulled on the pantry window, desperate to see what was going on outside.

It moved from the top, so he had to stretch as far as he could to get his fingers around the edge. He was in a panic, all reason gone, the only emotions left directed at survival.

He had to get out! At the very least, he had to see what was going on.

Carter stood in front of the massive wooden doors and thought.

Where was Chen? Did he have another escape route? If he did, he'd be long gone now. Carter moved to the side of a garden lily pond and slumped on a marble bench. What would he have done in the circumstances? Assuming he was rich beyond reason, and Chen was, he'd have had an elaborate escape route planned. It wouldn't be found until he was long gone.

Next, he'd set up a headquarters in a new location and it would be business as usual. And what was worse, since Chen had become totally dependent on electronics, he didn't have to be in Singapore or anywhere near it to control and expand his empire.

Carter shrugged, shook himself, fought off the pain from his wounds, shrapnel holes and burns that would have stopped a lesser man, and stood looking at the house.

One more try. He had to give it one more try.

He examined every door and window as he started from the front door and moved to the back. It was dark now. Examination of the structure was difficult. Lights were on in only a few windows but that didn't mean that anyone was inside.

At the back of the house, a light shone in a small window. It looked different somehow. A shadow appeared behind it, but the window was so grimy that Carter couldn't be sure of what he was seeing.

Suddenly he knew. He was looking into the face of a frightened Chinese man through a slightly opened window.

Carter's heart lurched as he reached for a grenade. The face in the window disappeared. Fingers clawed at the windowframe and it started to close.

The grenade was in Carter's hand. He had to move quickly, too fast to take careful aim. He wished now that he'd kept the cesta on his arm.

He pulled the quick release pin and let it fly. It hit the side of the frame and bounced back at him. His heart was in his mouth. He didn't have time to reach for another and the one on the ground at his feet could explode at any second.

Instinct took over. He picked up the grenade and tossed it underhand at the slight opening. Miraculously it passed between the bars, through the narrow opening, and exploded as soon as it was inside the structure.

• • •

Chen put down the cold lobster tail he'd just cracked and cocked an ear. Had the explosion been inside the house? Impossible.

But he smelled smoke. It didn't smell the same as the one that had exploded outside.

It was inside!

He threw the food on the tray and heaved himself up to a standing position, then he lumbered toward the room next door and the elevator that would take him to safety.

Heu Choy fell from the stool bounced to the far corner of the pantry as the small object exploded. He didn't see all the pieces of flaming material because he was blinded by the ball of fire that had appeared over his head.

But he felt the heat and smelled things burning. It was the tiles beside him, the table in the corner, and something else. He'd smelled it after a fire in town. Burning flesh.

He was on fire!

He smelled the burning flesh just seconds before he felt the excruciating pain. He screamed and scrambled to his feet. He ran from the pantry and down the back hall to the main dining room, lighting the way with his own body.

The heavy dining room drapes caught his eye first. He pulled them down and tried to roll in them to put out the fire. Some of the pieces of phosphorus dislodged and caught in the cloth. Heu Choy had to let one of the drapes go as it became a flaming torch.

The front doors. He had to get out.

He pulled at the latch of the doors and flung them open only to find himself trapped by steel bars.

He knew something about the bars. What was it? He'd been ordered to feed the contractors who had put the bars in. What had they told him?

"O God that looks over small Chinese men, let the pain go away so I can think!" he shouted to the night sky.

Power. They'd told him about the power. The doors were controlled by electromagnets that held them in place. He dropped the piece of drapery material, ran to a basement door, smoke trailing after him as the tiny bits of phosphorus ate into his flesh. The main power switch was just inside the basement door.

It was big and it was installed above his head. Frantically he ran to the hall for a chair and placed it beneath the master switch. Screaming from pain unlike anything he'd ever imagined, he swung from the large handle until it gave way and everything was plunged into darkness—except for the phosphorus eating away at him. It gave off an eerie glow that illuminated the cellar stairwell.

Heu Choy picked up the cloth again and ran to the front doors. He hadn't heard the metallic clang of all the steel bars as the magnets let go and the fingers of steel were yanked back into place by massive springs.

Facing the open sky and freedom, the little Chinese servant ran like a man possessed until he stumbled into the arms of a tall man he hadn't seen in the dark. Cradled in strong arms, the fiery pieces of chemical were pried from his flesh, and he was wrapped in the luxurious drapery.

It was the last thing he remembered before a darkness that was not of the night enfolded him.

Carter couldn't believe the luck that had come his way. After his lucky toss at the rear of the house, he'd made his way back to the front doors. He'd been there when the small Chinese man flung them open.

He reached into his apron pocket for another grenade when something told him to give it a moment. He held the grenade at the ready, not about to duplicate the near miss he'd just experienced. In less than a minute every set of steel bars clanged upward and the house was cast into complete darkness.

A feeling of triumph welled up in him. The knowledge that it might not be too late to carry out his mission made the adrenaline rush and he felt like a new man.

He had to act, decisively, and now. While the thought occurred, the small Chinese came flying out of the house and literally fell into his arms.

A servant. Probably one of Chen's slaves, Carter supposed.

The little man smelled of burning flesh. He'd been the one at the back of the house. Carter flipped Hugo into his hand and pried all the bits of phosphorus he could find out of the man's hide and wrapped him in the drapery material clutched in the man's hand. It was the best he could do and he couldn't afford one more minute.

Chen could be gone, probably was gone. Carter was glad now that he hadn't tossed more phosphorus grenades right away. If Chen had escaped, Carter knew he would have to find the escape route before the fire at the back of the house consumed everything.

He entered the front hall with care. He'd pulled the empty clip from his Luger and slapped in a fresh one. He held the Luger in his left hand and a grenade in the other. He could pull the quick-release pin with his teeth.

He heard nothing but the roar of flames from the back of the house. They were not loud yet but soon would be. He could feel the heat and smell the burning wood.

"Chen!" he called up the stairs. "Are you up there?"

He waited a minute and it seemed like an hour as smoke

started to pour from under the doors leading to the back of the house.

"Chen! If you're in there, I can take you out!"

"Help me, Carter! I've fallen and sprained my ankle. Some glass . . . I can't walk," the voice came back at him. It wasn't the booming, confident voice Carter had heard before, it was like the voice of a small, frightened child, but it was indeed Chen.

So he hadn't made it to an escape route. Carter quickly went through all possible scenarios in his mind. He couldn't lift Chen. The man would have to be able to help himself. While he helped Chen, he would be vulnerable. And if Chen were armed, the madman might be after a final revenge. In the few seconds he went over the possibilities, the fire at the back of the house raged out of control and lessened his options.

The fire broke through a door from the back of the house, making the decision for Carter. He pulled the pin from the grenade with his teeth and tossed it to the top of the stairs. He holstered his Luger and emptied the apron of grenades, tossing the small white explosives indiscriminately up the stairs and into adjoining rooms. Then he stumbled outside and sat on the marble bench next to the lily pond. The flames from the house changed the white lilies in the pond to red and orange. A kaleidoscopic nightmare of color filled the grounds around him.

One by one the bulletproof windows were blown out by the intense pressure from within. Wind tore at his clothing as a whirling column of fire drew air toward it from ground level. The heat intensified until it was almost unbearable but still he sat.

It wasn't over. It wasn't over until he knew, until he really knew.

An animal howl was torn from deep down in the lungs of the man inside. It was impossible that he could still be alive. No human could survive the inferno that sent flames a hundred feet into the sky.

He could hear the sirens now over the roar of the flames. The hair at the back of his hands curled and disappeared as he started to rise from the bench and meet Chief Windsor at the front gate.

From the heart of the fire a figure emerged. It lurched from side to side, blinded, its senses gone, a monster already dead but still on its feet.

Carter stared, fascinated, unable to take his eyes from the vision and unable to move from the heat that was intensifying.

It shuffled toward him, a tower of walking flame that peaked at the top and gave off smoke like some huge, round candle.

It came straight at Carter as if it had a destiny or some mad purpose. The Killmaster held his ground until Chen was within ten feet, then, with most of the hair singed below the edges of his helmet, he had to stand aside or be consumed.

The torch that had once been a human being stumbled on, tripped over the marble edging around the lily pond, and toppled in. Steam rose from the pool and gave off a stench that Carter would smell in his subconscious for many months to come. Every fire, every lighting of his Dunhill, every time he saw a lighted candle, would remind him of the monster of Singapore and the death of a very special lady.

He stepped back from the heat, moved no more than a dozen paces, saw the first police car, then allowed himself to collapse.

DON'T MISS THE NEXT NEW
NICK CARTER SPY THRILLER

RUBY RED DEATH

Carter skirted the lobby and signaled the bell captain to follow him toward the elevators.

"You need a doctor, senhor?"

"No. I need a bucket of ice and Senhor Ravel Bourlein's room number, pronto." He gave the man a bill and pushed the button for his floor.

In his room he repaired his face and examined the body bruises. The skin was already turning purple, but nothing was broken.

There was a rap on the door and he let the bellman in. "Bourlein?"

"He is in a suite, Twelve-twelve."

Carter gave him another hefty tip and shoved him out the door. He built a scotch and drank it while he changed clothes. Then he slipped the Beretta into his belt and took the elevator to the twelfth floor.

"Who is it?"

"Bell captain, senhor," Carter said, in a high voice. "You have a cable."

The door opened a crack and Carter shouldered it wide. He gave Bourlein two good shots in the middle of his flab and then a hard one behind the ear on his way down.

He kicked the door shut, locked it, and dragged the fat man by his ankles into the suite.

The woman, Nanette, stood naked except for a pair of bikini panties, her mouth round in a silent scream.

"Not a sound," Carter growled. "Get some ice and a wet towel."

She nodded dumbly, eyes bulging, and moved into the small kitchen area.

"Move it!" Carter barked. "I'm in a hurry."

The woman had gotten her breath and a little nerve back. "What the hell do you want?"

"A little talk with him . . . bring the stuff."

She returned, her vast bosoms jiggling and swaying. She tried a hesitant smile, but one look at Carter's face and she cut the act and thrust the ice and the wet towel at him.

"Over here," Carter said.

To her astonishment, Carter gathered a fistful of Bourlein's shirtfront and jerked him to a sitting position, then lifted him into a chair. He motioned her around behind the chair.

"Rub the back of his neck with the ice."

"Let me get some clothes on,—" she whimpered.

Carter looked at her, stepped forward, and slapped her. She went sideways, airborne. Her vision dimmed with stars behind her eyes. She felt herself jerked upright by her hair, held there by the aching, stinging strain on her scalp until her wobbly knees found strength and she stood. Just as she got her wind, the throbbing pain along the left side of her face began occupying her mind. She tried twisting away and the grip in her hair tightened. Carter slapped her again, and she shrieked.

"No, no!" she cried.

"Good," Carter said, "I don't like it either." He turned loose his grip wound in her long dark hair and shoved. She stumbled across the room and fell in Bourlein's lap.

"Up!" he hissed, and she shot to her feet. "Use that ice on the back of his neck."

She squealed and sprawled as she reached for the ice, got it, and scrambled to her feet. She tilted Bourlein's head forward and began rubbing his neck with the ice.

Carter went to work on his face with the towel, back and forth, one side, then the other. Bourlein began moving, then moaning. Finally he cried out and jerked upright.

"What the—" he gasped.

Carter's face was inches from his. "Three bad local lads tried to bust my head tonight," he hissed.

"I don't know anything about it . . ."

"You ass. You tried to make a deal. I didn't dance. So you tried to put me in a hospital so I couldn't be there to make a bid."

"You're crazy."

"I don't think so," Carter said. "You had Big Boobs here call the lads from the restaurant and give them my description. There was no deal. You just wanted to get me out of the way."

"No, I swear . . ."

"Bullshit." Carter looked up at the trembling woman. "Right?"

She gulped and then nodded, once.

Carter dropped the towel, drew the Beretta, and crammed the barrel between Bourlein's fat lips, shattering teeth. The man reared back and the woman squealed.

Carter shot her a look, and she quieted instantly.

"You hear me, Bourlein? Blink your eyes if you do," he growled.

Bourlein blinked. He tried leaning forward, making gagging sounds.

"Swallow it," Carter commanded. "Swallow it all, you bastard." He rammed the gun barrel hard, feeling the high, ribbed front sight rip the roof of Bourlein's mouth, rammed until the trigger guard rested against his fat lips, inches of cold steel gun barrel gagging him, choking him, his eyes bulging.

The woman kept making tiny mewling sounds, like those of a kitten in pain.

"Let me give you your itinerary for the next few hours, fat man. You're going to call the desk and have them get you a car. Then you're going to check out and you're going to drive to São Paolo. Bolivar's watchdogs will follow you. They won't know what's going on, and by the time they figure it out you and Nanny here will be on the first flight. You got that? I don't give a shit where the flight goes, just so it's out of the country and you're on it. Nod if you understand."

Bourlein didn't move. He just stared pure hate at Carter from his beady eyes.

The Killmaster cocked his Beretta. "So long, fat man."

The head started nodding.

Carter wiped the barrel on Bourlein's shirt, stuck the gun back in his belt, and headed for the door, where he paused.

"If I see you at Rancho Corinto, Bourlein, I'll kill you."

He took the elevator to the fourth floor and knocked on 417. He heard the padding of bare feet and then Verna Rashkin's sleepy voice.

"Who is it?"

"Fabian Huzel. Open up."

The door opened and Carter slid inside. She backed away and he kicked it closed. Her hair was tousled and she wore only a sheer black nightgown, low in front, that stopped at midthigh. Under the black garment's gauzy transparency, her smooth pink-and-whiteness gleamed and shimmered as she moved. The black material rustled around her, more like a dark mist than a cover, heightening her nakedness rather than concealing it. But in the end her flesh glowed with blinding incandescence.

"What do you want?" she whispered.

"You made a proposition a little while ago. Is it still on?"

Suddenly she was bright-eyed and alert. "It is."

"Then you've got a deal," Carter said.

"You won't regret it. I'll get Bourlein's bid as soon as we get to Rancho Corinto."

"From Nanette?"

Her eyes narrowed. "How did you know?"

"I didn't," Carter said. "I guessed. You'd never get to Bourlein. It had to be his whore."

She shrugged. "Nanette's tired of him, and I offered her a good retirement plan."

"I upped your offer," Carter said. "Bourlein won't be bidding. It's all ours."

She couldn't conceal her surprise. "How did you do that?"

"Proper conversation," Carter said. "Aren't you forgetting something?"

"What?"

"The rest of your offer."

Her lips parted showing sharp, white teeth. "All night,"

she whispered. "I'm going to make love to you all night."

Her hands slid down her thighs, to the hem of the nightie just above her knees. Still moving slowly, she raised it, revealing her long, slender legs inch by quivering inch. When it was at a point just below the juncture of her legs, she swayed her body around so that her back was to him. The nightie inched up higher and now he could see the firm, high globes of her buttocks. Her rhythmical movement quickened. The muscles of her derrière rippled and the flesh began to jump with a sort of erotic frenzy.

Then she quickly pulled the garment over her head, flipped it away, and turned to face him.

He let his eyes roam over her body, at the firmness and maturity of her breasts, the sweeping curve of her hips. She seemed to delight in feeling his eyes on her, for she lifted her long hair with the tips of her fingers and turned around slowly, displaying herself.

"Well?" she murmured.

"Nice," Carter said, "damn nice. See you in the morning."

"What?" she cried.

"Just wanted to see if your word was good," he said over his shoulder as he let himself out. "'Night."